Eric Ambler was born int(
years helped out as a pι
engineering as a full time ca.___, aιιιιough this quickly gave way to
writing. In World War II he entered the army and looked likely to
fight in the line, but was soon after commissioned and ended the war
as assistant director of the army film unit and a Lieutenant-Colonel.

This experience translated into civilian life and Ambler had a very
successful career as a screen writer, receiving an Academy Award for
his work on *The Cruel Sea* by Nicolas Monsarrat in 1953. Many of his
own works have been filmed, the most famous probably being *Light
of Day*, filmed as *Topkapi* under which title it is now published.

He established a reputation as a thriller writer of extraordinary
depth and originality and received many other accolades during his
lifetime, including two *Edgar Awards* from *The Mystery Writers of
America* (best novel for *Topkapi* and best biographical work for *Here
Lies Eric Ambler),* and two *Gold Dagger Awards* from the *Crime Writer's
Association (Passage of Arms* and *The Levanter).*

Often credited as being the inventor of the modern political
thriller, *John Le Carre* once described Ambler as '*the source on which we
all draw.*' A recurring theme in his works is the success of the well
meaning yet somewhat bungling amateur who triumphs in the face
of both adversity and hardened professionals.

Ambler wrote under his own name and also during the 1950's a
series of novels as *Eliot Reed*, with *Charles Rhodda*. These are now
published under the '*Ambler*' umbrella.

Works of **ERIC AMBLER** published by
HOUSE OF STRATUS

DOCTOR FRIGO
JUDGMENT ON DELTCHEV
THE LEVANTER
THE SCHIRMER INHERITANCE
THE SIEGE OF THE VILLA LIPP   (Also as 'Send No More Roses')
TOPKAPI   (Also as 'The Light Of Day')

Originally as Eliot Reed with Charles Rhodda:
CHARTER TO DANGER
THE MARAS AFFAIR
PASSPORT TO PANIC
TENDER TO DANGER   (Also as 'Tender To Moonlight')
SKYTIP

Passport to Panic

eric Ambler

(Writing as Eliot Reed with Charles Rhodda)

HOUSE OF
STRATUS

This edition published in 2010 by House of Stratus, an imprint of
Stratus Books Ltd., Lisandra House, Fore Street,
Looe, Cornwall, PL13 1AD, U.K.

www.houseofstratus.com

Typeset, printed and bound by House of Stratus.

A catalogue record for this book is available from the British Library and the Library
of Congress.

ISBN 0-7551-2540-1
EAN 978-0-7551-2540-1

CHAPTER I

LEWIS PAGE waited all the afternoon for a cable from San Mateo. At six o'clock he telephoned Western Union, but there was nothing for him. He gave the clerk his home number, requesting that any message should be relayed to him.

"It's most urgent," he explained. "From my brother, Mr. Julian Page, of the Casa Alta, Rosario Province."

The detail would, perhaps, underline the urgency, but he knew that it was unnecessary. It came involuntarily from his swiftly increasing anxiety.

He stared at the blotter on his desk, but what he saw was an aerial perspective of the little republic of San Mateo: the sand-fringe of the Pacific Coast, the long wharves of Santa Teresa, the palm-bordered plaza of Trajano. He closed his eyes. His anxieties were like the tangled jungle that washed up against the hills of the coffee plantations.

A noise at the door brought him back. Talliver, his partner, looked at him concernedly, with something a little patronising in his commiseration; or so it seemed to the elder man. Talliver had the superior attitude of one who accepts the inevitable. He shook his head slowly.

"No reply?"

It was a comment more than a question.

"Not yet." Lewis Page held desperately to hope.

"What's the use? Why should Julian put up his money to save us?"

"You don't know Julian. He's not the sort to refuse me. Anything he has is mine. It has always been like that between us."

"Goodness, man, you've tried him, haven't you? Three letters by air-mail. No reply. Two cables. No reply."

"There's something wrong."

"Yes, there's something wrong. We're smashed, and Julian has better use for his cash than to pour it into a bankrupt concern."

"I explained everything in my first letter. A safe loan for a few months, to carry us over."

"A bagatelle! A mere ten thousand! It's on the way, no doubt, by ordinary mail. He just hasn't had time to write out a cable. Too much to do round the hacienda, and the help have been out picking coffee. I understand they pick coffee all the year round at his altitude."

"Damn it, Bob, you don't have to sneer. He's my brother."

"Does that make him a fool?" Talliver repeated the slow shake of his head. "You'd better resign yourself, Lewis."

"What's the matter with you?" Lewis flared in indignation. "Don't you want to fight?"

Talliver made a protesting noise. "I've fought all I know, and my last penny is in the kitty. Do you think I'm any more delighted than you are with the prospect of losing everything? I have a wife and two growing boys. You've only yourself and Anne, and you've Julian to turn to. He may be tight with his cash, but no doubt he'll welcome you on the old plantation. The next time he digs up one of his stone gods, you'll be in on it. That will be exciting."

Lewis ignored the bitterness. "There's something wrong," he insisted.

Talliver shrugged. "I've finished for the day. You'd better come along with me. I'll buy you a drink."

"No. Not yet."

Lewis had a decision to make and Talliver could not help him. A few minutes ago he had been eager to reach home, but impatience had gone with the end of expectation. There would be no message from San Mateo.

Street lamps glowed through a thickening dusk. Alone, Lewis paced from the window to the door and back again. When he looked from the window, he could see half the dome of St. Paul's in a slot between two tall buildings. He turned again and took his hat from the stand in the corner. He hesitated with hand on the door-knob. Then he decided.

Throwing his hat on the desk, he pulled the phone towards him and dialled.

"Mr. Darren, please."

He waited.

"Darren? This is Page. I have to get to Trajano as soon as possible. I want you to book me on the first available plane."

"Trajano? That's San Mateo. Which route?"

"Any route, so long as I don't lose time. There's always someone cancelling at the last minute, isn't there?"

"Not always. How about your visa?"

"I can get it as soon as the Consul opens in the morning."

"Money?" Darren thought of everything.

"I'll see my bank. They can fix it by cable if necessary. Anyway, my brother's out there. I shall not be worried about immediate funds. The important thing is to be on the way."

"How soon can you leave?"

"As soon as a plane can take me. Is there a flight round eleven?"

"In the morning? You're certainly in a hurry. How long do you expect to be in San Mateo? What about that holiday cruise with your daughter?"

Lewis jerked his head nervously. He had forgotten.

"You'll have to cancel it. Things have come up unexpectedly. I must see my brother in San Mateo at once. Do your best for me, please. Phone me at the house to-night as soon as you have news. I'll be home within an hour."

The traffic on the way to Richmond was heavy, and he chafed whenever the lights held him up. Normally he would have put the car away in the garage as soon as he got home. To-night he left it at the kerb and hurried up the path to the front door. Almost from the moment that he had started from the office, renewed hope had raised the prospect that the cable company might be trying to reach him. A reply from Julian would put everything right, and surely it must come. When he thought of the urgency of his last message, hope became certainty. There would be no need for him to dash off across the world.

"Has anyone telephoned?"

His housekeeper shook her head. No one had telephoned. Except a young man for Anne.

"They're always ringing her up. Not that it does them any good." Mrs. Benson put a note of deprecation into it. Young girls should not be so resolutely unresponsive to the calls of romance.

"Where is Anne?" her father asked.

"It's her late night at that old music school, Mr. Page. I've held up dinner as usual. It's a good thing the term ends next week. The way she works, the holidays won't come too soon for her. If anyone needs a good sea voyage to put a bit of colour in her cheeks, she does."

The words were a reproach to him. The great days that he and Anne had planned and talked over for months had been wiped out by one word to Darren. The restful voyage, the Piraeus, the isles of Greece, then Naples and Rome – all cancelled. To-night he would have to explain, and he dreaded the girl's disappointment. When he returned from San Mateo, he would be up to his neck in business, setting things straight.

He poured himself a drink. From the wall above the cocktail cabinet the enlarged photograph of Julian's first stone god leered grotesquely down at him, its set of even teeth seemingly clamped together by two pairs of fearsome, interlocking fangs. Not a comfortable household idol, rather an angry, menacing projection of a primitive people's terror; yet, by a queer twist, it was indirectly responsible for a way of life that had brought prosperity to Julian.

"Treat the old boy with respect," Julian had urged. "He will see that your enterprises flourish. He will look after you as he has looked after me."

The laugh and the jocular manner did not abate the suggestion that the archaeologist had acquired something of the superstition of the people among whom he lived. To Lewis the stone image had always seemed a contradictory symbol. It was a strange supposition that benevolence could come from a thing that wore such a mask of evil.

But Julian himself was a figure of contradictions: a fantastic, a reckless visionary with an overruling talent for the practical. How madly he had cut loose when he received his share of old William Page's estate! No more browsing in museums or poking round Cornish hillsides for ancient hut-clusters. He would throw up his job and go in search of those gods that had been his pet study since he had, as a boy, progressed from Rider Haggard to Prescott. He would go to the Aztecs, to the Incas, to the Mayas.

He went. For years he wandered in Honduras, Yucatan, Guatemala, Mexico, Colombia. He saw and studied the discoveries of other archaeologists. He ended up in San Mateo, and there in the hills he unearthed his own god, ten tons of grotesquely carved rock. When he wanted to buy it and take it away, the native owner of the ground had said no. *Todos diablos,* no! It was one thing to dig up a god, but to move it from its home place was to invite misfortune. The ten plagues, including leprosy, would descend upon the unfaithful custodian.

The credulous one had been quite specific about leprosy.

"Then," Julian had said, "if you will sell me your plot, I will be the custodian and you will have nothing to fear."

Neither the logic nor the proffered pesos could be rejected. In another week Julian had become a landowner and everyone was satisfied; the god included, presumably, since he was not to be disturbed in his tenancy.

A mad act, but quite characteristic.

Lewis, with his drink untasted, turned from the god to a camera portrait on a side table. This was Julian, the impulsive, the generous, who would spend his last peso to acquire a bit of earth with a god in it, who would mortgage everything he possessed to help a friend.

Something must have gone wrong.

Lewis forgot his own case in his anxiety over his brother. He stared at the portrait as if to compel an explanation from it, but the eyes of Julian, always with the light of humour in them, smiled at him, and the lift of the head, with the dark mass of hair tossed back, was in the gesture of one about to give way to laughter. So he had looked, telling his own strange tale, on his last visit to England three years ago.

"And a week after I bought the place, my nearest neighbour came to the shack. 'There is a god on my property,' he said. 'My son has married in Trajano and I am thinking of joining him. I will sell cheap, not like that rogue Carlos. My land is good land. When the jungle is cleared, you can plant coffee.' So I bought another god, and that was the beginning of my finca, my plantation. I didn't know a thing about coffee, but I had to do something. The pesos were running out. Now – well, I own the whole hillside and there are nine gods and two warriors on the front lawn."

Julian had laughed, throwing back that thick head of hair, and Lewis, thinking of the trick, wondered that Julian had never grown old. Years ago the brothers had been similar in appearance, except that Julian had been taller and lankier. Now other differences were marked. Lewis, the stay-at-home, the cautious, was beginning to show his years. His hair had thinned a little and there were touches of grey in it, and it was only by persistent exercise that he could keep his body in reasonable shape. He had buried a wife and brought up a daughter. He had promoted companies and made money out of ingenious gadgets. He had walked carefully and never far from home, and now he was bankrupt and looking for salvation from the brother who had always been too busy with his own whims and fancies to think of marriage.

A confirmed bachelor, Julian. Or a dedicated romantic. There had been an affair and a disappointment long ago, and this, perhaps, was the key to his wanderings and his avoidance of women. Yet, adoring Anne, he had sometimes been jealous of his brother's good fortune in such a possession.

Lewis recalled the last disturbing farewell.

"I hope you thank heaven for Anne," Julian had said. "I do. She'll come in for all I own when I shuffle off. Don't let her want for anything while I'm alive, Lewis. If you strike trouble at all, let me know at once."

The remembered words accented anxiety in Lewis. He put aside his drink and went to the telephone.

"I'm sorry, Mr. Page," the Western Union clerk told him. "Nothing has come through from San Mateo."

CHAPTER II

SHE HAD GROWN up so faithfully in the image of her mother that he was sometimes reminded too bitterly of the loss her birth had caused him. In her infancy he had often looked on her with resentment. She was a stranger from whom he must withdraw; a stranger to be handed over to the care of one hired woman after another. Although ever scrupulous about her well-being, he could not now think of those days without reproaching himself. He had been selfish in his grief, but he had long since made up for the fault by unremitting devotion.

Anne had become the one reason for his existence, yet she had her own life to make, and he was constantly worried by her dependence on him, fearing that he had bound her too closely to him. He was aware that, away from him, she was an isolate, retreating upon herself, finding an outlet only in her music.

To-night she came in moodily, scowling over some thought. The manner in which she threw her brief-case on to the settee told him that her composition lesson had not gone so well. She was dejected, but her eyes took a new light when she saw him, as if he had a charm to remove her cares. She had the clear blue eyes of her mother, but the shadows sometimes in them were her own. She had her mother's fine profile, the same soft, waved hair, almost flaxen, though she wore it in a different style, drawn back to a pony tail that bobbed to every nervous dart of her head. Drawn back too carelessly.

He was troubled that she never made the most of herself. It was the same with her dress. He took pains to see that she had good clothes, but everything she wore quickly showed the strains of casual use. She was happy only in jeans and a boyish shirt, and they inevitably took from her fingers the smudges and ink stains that seemed inseparable from her work.

"Look at your hands," he reproved her, as she hurried to him.

"Sorry," she answered. "It's that wretched pen. I'll wash."

The phone rang while she was on her way upstairs.

Darren said: "There's not a seat on a plane until to-morrow afternoon. I'm booking you to New York and arranging connections to Santa Teresa through Cristobal. I understand there's a train from the port to Trajano, but it's slow."

"I know all about that," Lewis told him. "I've been there. I can get a local plane to Trajano. When do I leave London Airport?"

"Some time after lunch. I have to check up in the morning. I'll have the tickets and time-table for you first thing."

Anne came down, spruced up a little.

"You didn't put your car away," she remarked. "Are you going out to-night?"

"No." Lewis was conscious of a tightness in his voice. Now that the journey had been arranged, he saw the enormity of it.

"What's the matter, Father?" Anne demanded. "You look frightened."

"Not frightened." He managed to smile. Then he told her of his decision. He was anxious about Uncle Julian, he said. He had written, cabled . . .

"There's something else," she insisted. "You've been worried for days. You've never bothered about Uncle Julian before, even when you've had to wait months for a letter. You've always been sure of him."

"This time I'm not sure." He hesitated. "I have to see him. I need his help. We're in a little trouble at the office. Nothing much. We formed a company to put a new article on the market, but . . . In short, you wouldn't understand the details." He grimaced, closing his eyes. "It's a case of a patent infringement. We thought everything was clear."

"Is it that refrigerator business?"

"Yes. We're faced with rather a loss."

"You can use my money."

8

"Not on any account. That was from your mother, for yourself."
He smiled, pressing her arm. "Besides, it isn't enough. Not nearly.
Don't you worry. Uncle Julian will lend me all I need. I'm afraid,
though, we'll have to postpone our little holiday."

The effort it took her to cover her dismay was plain.

"Perhaps we'll be able to go in the winter," he added.

"I don't mind, Father. Really, I don't."

He knew how acutely she did mind. She had been full of
preparations, reading everything she could get hold of about Athens
and the islands, marking in guidebooks the places she must see in Italy:
the opera houses, the haunts and monuments of the great in music.
And more than anything she had looked forward to the sea voyage.

"We'll talk about it when I get back," he said. "There may still be
time to fix up something."

He was awake most of the night, blaming himself again and again
for her disappointment, and in the morning he returned to the
alleviating argument. She must not give up hope.

"It's really best that I should stay at home," she answered him. "I still
have a lot of work to do on my string quartet. Max will give me some
private lessons."

"I'd rather have you find something else to do." He frowned
unhappily. "Don't you get enough of your music during the term?"

"Enough music!" She laughed. "Don't be absurd, Father."

She poured coffee into his cup. "How happy Uncle Julian will be
to see you." The thought brought a longing to her eyes. "I wish I
could go with you. I've heard so much about his Casa Alta, I sometimes
dream of it. What a wonderful place it must be. Some day you must
take me there."

Julian had always wanted that.

"Some day, no doubt." Lewis frowned, turning his gaze from her.
"If only I hadn't to rush off at such short notice . . ."

CHAPTER III

THE THOUGHT went with him, nagging him on every stage of the trip. Impossible to have taken her in the circumstances, of course. But this, perhaps, was the dictate of London, where life was conditioned by the account books in a stodgy office and everything a little out of the ordinary was impossible.

By the time his plane was circling over Santa Teresa, waiting for the signal to come in, the impossible had become the feasible. San Mateo was very far from England, and the Lewis Page who watched the wheeling cyclorama of sea and sky and mountains was even more remote from the man who had laboured for years with Bob Talliver to achieve bankruptcy.

Here was a climate of exhilaration and hope, and this was a flight to freedom. Lewis Page was out of his prison, and, in long perspective, the routine of the city and the humdrum affairs of a suburban home seemed infinitely dreary. Of course, he had endured everything for Anne's sake, but where had it got him? And where was it getting Anne?

The spirit of the girl was as subdued as his own had been. She might do something as a composer, something that would give her satisfaction, but it was more important that she should become a woman. Perhaps she had a loveliness that needed no adornment, but he wanted to see in her more of her mother's femininity; at least some little thought of feminine things.

He had, on occasions, given her modest pieces of jewellery, but heaven alone knew what she did with them. Recently he had been quite annoyed because she had mislaid an emerald ring that Julian had had made for her, and only his insistence had kept her searching till it was found.

"Such a fuss about a bit of old glass," she had complained, repeating Julian's own description of the stone. But it was something that Julian himself had uncovered in the hills of Rosario, and she should have valued it as his gift, especially as he had gone to a lot of trouble over the setting.

Something had to be done about Anne; something to bring her out of her own peculiar prison. And here, in this New World, was the climate. If it could give him a sense of his own importance, take years off his shoulders, make him feel that he was still alive . . .

He looked at the woman across the gangway.

A very beautiful woman, beautifully groomed.

From the moment she boarded the plane at Cristobal he had been thinking how attractive she was. Again and again he had taken his eyes off her by a conscious effort, self-reproving, only to find his gaze returning a moment or two later. When other passengers were eager for a first glimpse of the Cordilleras, he looked only at that exquisite face with the warm-tinted olive skin and the large dark eyes.

Turning from her, he stared at the air-line leaflet in his hand. He must connect with the Trajano plane at Santa Teresa. He read the pertinent paragraph over and over, but the words made no sense to him. He thought of the life he had led, bounded by his devotion to a memory, but could find no satisfaction in it any longer. It was false. It had been nothing but a defeat.

Hang it all, he was not so old. He was even a year younger than Julian. To deny life at forty was insane. To tell himself that he was finished was just emotional and physical indolence. If he took himself in hand, there was still a prospect of living. Anne was fast growing up. Soon she would look beyond herself, and in the normal course would marry. Then he would be alone; but only in another degree, for he was alone already, with no contact that could take him out of his indolence.

It might be that this woman across the gangway was similarly alone, needing friendship. He had only to reach out to touch her shoulder or take her hand, but she was unaware of him, and they must go on as strangers.

11

She turned at that moment and he could look into her eyes. It seemed that she gazed directly at him, but he knew that she was still unaware of him, passing him with a casual glance. There was sadness in her face, and something else that he could not exactly define; a nervousness, even fear, but it was probably no more than an apprehensiveness of the little worries at a journey's end.

In another moment the plane touched down and she descended to the runway just ahead of him. A man met her in the terminal building, but there was no hint of intimacy in the encounter, not even the offer of a gloved hand from the woman.

Lewis watched the two go off together. He was deprived, desolate, halted uncertainly in the middle of the wide hall. Then he shook himself out of the mood. He was being absurd, and he had no time to be absurd. He had to think of Trajano and Julian. He went quickly towards the inquiry counter, only to be told that he had missed the connection for the capital, and there was but one flight daily.

He looked out from the hall upon the sprawling mass of the mountain range that barred access to the central valley. He could take the night train that crawled and squirmed and panted a hard way up and through and across the barrier, but he would save no time by doing so. He decided to wait for the next day's plane.

Since no reply had come from the Casa Alta to his several messages from London, he had planned to surprise Julian by walking in on him, but, now that he was so close, impatience to see his brother made him send a telegram with the news that he would be on the plane. That would be surprise enough. That would start Julian off at an early hour in the morning on the long drive down from the highlands to Trajano. He could imagine how excited Julian would be at the airport. And Julian's regret that Anne had been left in London.

It was a regret that Lewis himself began to feel acutely, and later, when he gazed from a balcony of the Hotel Granada at the busy scene presented by the harbour, he was further troubled by the thought. How Anne would have loved all this! Instead, cheated of her holiday, she would be moping at home, quarrelling with the too motherly Mrs. Benson, no doubt.

The imagined picture brought him to an impulsive decision worthy of Julian himself. Anne should have her voyage. For the isles of Greece he would substitute other islands: Bermuda, the Bahamas, Cuba. Then there would be the ports of the Canal and of the West Coast down to Santa Teresa, where he would meet her, and Julian, of course, would be with him at the dockside.

All this would involve a delay of three or four weeks at least in his return to London, but time no longer seemed important. While waiting for Anne he would be enjoying himself at the Casa Alta. Once a loan was arranged and the money transferred, Talliver could handle things in London.

He paused a moment in the foyer. He had heard whispers of trouble; political trouble, insurrection. But there was always talk of insurrection in San Mateo. It was a popular pastime, congenital; an expression of the intense partisanship that gave an edge to existence and boosted the circulation of the factional newspapers. Sometimes there had been a little shooting, but a stable government now ruled and, even in the remote contingency of violence, there was no risk if you kept off the streets.

Lewis called for cable forms. Later he posted an airmail letter to Anne, explaining everything, and his sense of well-being was brought to perfection. In the dining room that night he looked at the guests, hoping that he might see again the woman who had been a fellow passenger from Cristobal, but disappointment in this could not diminish his cheerfulness. He laughed at himself.

The feeling of pleasurable living remained with him all the evening. His fear that something might be wrong with his brother was forgotten, but it came back to him when he stepped from the plane at Trajano airport next day. Julian was not there to meet him.

CHAPTER IV

THE NIGHT cable-letter from San Mateo was quite clear, though to Anne, in the first impact, it was unbelievable. A fairy story, a dream, reduced to commonplace terms. She was to pack at once, take a plane to New York, and go on by steamer to Santa Teresa. Mr. Darren would attend to the bookings and all the other arrangements.

"But it's impossible," Anne complained nervously.

"It's there in black and white, isn't it?" Mrs. Benson was indignant with her. "What's impossible about it?"

"I can't go all that way alone. I'd get lost."

"Rubbish! You got a tongue in your head to ask the way, haven't you? You can speak English of a sort, and you've been learning Spanish."

"But school doesn't end till next week."

"All these years you've been wanting to go to your Uncle Julian. Now you can't give up a few days of your term! Let me tell you, miss, the sooner you're away from that old music, the better. If you were a daughter of mine, you'd be brought up proper, instead of messing your life away at banging a piano and scribbling crotchets and what-nots, working yourself into a decline. You go and phone up that Mr. Darren, like your father says."

Mr. Darren was expecting the call. He asked her to come in with her passport.

When she saw him in the afternoon, he was reassuring. Everything would be quite easy for her, but she must be prepared to leave in two days' time, as there was a chance of getting her a passage on the *Atacama*, a new motor vessel. He had already reserved a seat on a flight to New York, where his agent would look after her and put her on board the ship.

Mr. Darren, an old friend of the family, discussed her wardrobe warningly because of the climatic changes she would have to face. Anne went shopping in panic. By the time she arrived home, Mrs. Benson had already packed a suitcase and was busy marshalling the smaller effects.

"What have you done with your emerald ring?" the housekeeper demanded. "Have you lost it again? You can't go visiting your uncle without that ring. What would he think of you?"

"Why should he think anything? Stop fussing."

"I'd like to know what would become of you if someone didn't fuss." Mrs. Benson wheeled abruptly, swooped towards the bed, and picked up a wrinkled frock. "Look at this, for instance."

"What's the matter with it?"

"Matter enough. Crushed in among your clothes till it's creased and rumpled out of recognition. Your new party dress! I suppose I'll have to press it for you."

"Put it away. I shan't need it."

"Indeed you will need it. What do you think you're going to wear on that old boat? There'll be dancing and doings every night."

"Not for me. I hate dancing."

"You'll wear this frock, anyway. I suppose you think you can show up for dinner in your old blue jeans?"

"I will if I want to. Put the thing down and make me a cup of tea."

"A disgrace! That's what it is! A fine dress that cost pounds and pounds, and you don't know how to look after it."

"Are you going to get me a cup of tea, or do I have to make it myself?"

"You keep out of my kitchen." Mrs. Benson put menace into her voice, then, seeing the clock on the mantelpiece, changed her tone. "My goodness me! It can't be six already! You mean to tell me you haven't had your tea?"

CHAPTER V

IT WAS FIVE HOURS earlier in Trajano, and Lewis Page, hungry and exasperated, was wondering when he was going to get his lunch. He was having trouble with an official whom he took to be an immigration inspector, and his Spanish, long unused, was woefully unable to meet the demands put upon it.

"Your passport, please!"

That was easy enough both to understand and to answer. It was also easy enough to aver what should have been patent to anyone glancing at the personal information clearly set out. But question followed question, and the more he stammered and hesitated, the more excited and unintelligible the examiner became. Incomprehensible demands were fired at Lewis and repeated before he could turn a page in his phrase-book.

Another official, attracted by the noise, came to the counter and stared at him as if mentally calculating his anthropometric measurements. He took the passport from his colleague, squinted at the unflattering photograph of the victim, shook his head, and muttered something.

"Isn't there anyone here who understands English?" Lewis mopped his sweating brow. "Interpreter!" he demanded. "Interpreter!"

"*Intérprete,*" the second official corrected him academically, and went on with his muttering.

"Can I be of service, sir?"

The voice was politely inquiring, with a transatlantic emphasis on the "sir."

Lewis turned to face a tall, lean man of middle age, immaculate in tussore suit and wearing a broad-brimmed panama hat.

"It's very good of you, señor. I'm most grateful."

With the help of the volunteer interpreter the examination proceeded swiftly, but its purpose was still incomprehensible to the flustered Lewis.

"This is a new passport, issued two months ago?"

Lewis lifted his shoulders, but obliged with the redundant affirmative.

"Have you any other passport?"

"Of course not. You have to surrender the old one to get a new one."

"How many visits have you made to San Mateo in the last fifteen months?"

"Not any. This is the first since I was here ten years ago.

"Why did you come here ten years ago?"

"To see my brother."

"What is your business this time?"

"The same. Purely personal."

"Where is your brother?"

"That's what I would like to know," Lewis confided in his rescuer. "I expected him to meet me here, but he hasn't turned up."

The questions went on and on. What business was he engaged in, in London? How long had he stayed in New York? What contacts had he made there? Did he meet anyone in Cristobal? Was it not true that he had been in touch with a man calling himself Juan Perez?

Lewis sighed. "I've never heard of the man. I met nobody in Cristobal. What is all this about?"

The two officials muttered together confidentially and thumped the passport in turn.

"Be patient," the rescuer advised. "I think they are coming to the conclusion that you are not the man they took you for."

"Not the man! I'm Lewis Page. Isn't that clear to them?"

The stranger stroked a greying goatee that finished off his long sun-browned face. His dark eyes showed a light of amusement that might have been ironic.

"Hush!" he urged.

17

The questioning was resumed.

"Who is this brother of yours?"

"His name is Julian Page."

"What is his business in San Mateo?"

"He has a coffee plantation in the Rosario district."

More muttering. An interpolation by the stranger. Then:

"This Julian Page: he is the archaeologist?"

"Si, si, the archaeologist."

Si, si, si, si, si . . . The sibilants hissed, a pencil scratched the officials smiled and murmured apologies.

"I just don't understand," Lewis complained. "Did they take me for some sort of criminal?"

"A gun-runner, probably." The stranger again stroked his goatee and was even more amused. "We are all a little nervous about the Bartolistas, so you must excuse official curiosity in the line of duty. Perhaps you are not acquainted with the local situation, sir. The exiled Enrique Bartol has never given up hope of regaining the presidency. A lamentable fellow, our Enriquito, but persistent. There are rumours: a fifth column, agents coming and going, an insurrectionary air force harboured by one of our despicable neighbours. Perhaps there is nothing in any of it, but our worthy government sometimes shakes in its shoes."

The stranger laughed, displaying even rows of gleaming teeth. "I am glad I was able to extricate you from our politics," he added.

"I'm deeply in your debt." Lewis offered his hand. "May I know your name?"

"Balaguer." The rescuer bowed slightly. "Mauricio Balaguer y Lucientes. At your service. It seems we are joined in disappointment, Mr. Page. You expected to be met by your brother. I expected to meet a friend. He was not on the plane, so perhaps he has been arrested as a gun-runner." Señor Balaguer enjoyed his little joke. "What will you do now, sir?"

"I don't know." Lewis scowled uncertainly. "I had better wait a while. There may have been an accident. A flat tyre or something. It's a long road from Rosario. I think I should telephone."

"I, too, must call a number. Perhaps you would like me to get through to your brother's place for you?"

Lewis could not dream of putting him to the trouble, but it was no trouble at all to a man like Señor Balaguer y Lucientes who knew the tricks of the exchanges as well as the peculiarities of the local idiom. Alas, after an extended encounter with the telephone department in rapid-fire Spanish, he had to report that the Rosario line was out of order and no calls were being accepted.

"It happens in San Mateo," he apologised, and Lewis, waiting while his new friend made his own call, began to think that anything might happen in San Mateo.

The intense heat was more than troublesome to one unaccustomed to it. He looked anxiously up and down the long hall of the airport building, but no hurrying figure of Julian appeared to comfort him.

"Now," Señor Balaguer said, "we must consider what to do. If you start at once for Rosario, you might miss your brother on the way. Undoubtedly, when he finds he is too late for the airport, he will go to the Europa. Everybody goes to the Europa, so that is where he will expect to find you. We will leave word here with the inquiry officer. Then my car is at your service."

The lean, brown-faced fairy godfather had assumed full sponsorship. Lewis was beyond resistance, but at the Europa he insisted that his friend should take lunch with him. Before Señor Balaguer left, he offered further advice and the telephone number of a car-hire man who spoke English.

"But wait a little while," he urged. "Your brother may yet arrive. It has been a great pleasure to make your acquaintance. Perhaps we shall meet again some day. Who knows? Meanwhile I must be on my way. *Au revoir,* Mr. Page. *Hasta la vista.*"

Lewis sat in the foyer of Trajano's premier hotel and waited. Through the open, colonnaded front, he looked out across the Plaza with its old herring-bone pavement and its Bolivar in bronze. The palms in front of the Municipal Theatre drooped in a parched, complaining way, as if the heat were too much for them.

The watcher dabbed at his sweating brow and shifted in his cane chair. Movement was agonising. Gluey garments seemed to rip strips from suffering flesh.

Three o'clock, and still no Julian! Lewis eased the strap of his wrist-watch. He gazed at the ineffectual long-bladed fans that whispered faintly as they revolved overhead. He raised himself gingerly from the chair and walked out under the high-arched colonnade, but it was no cooler there.

Trajano, or at any rate the Plaza, was little changed in ten years, except that a new block of offices had gone up on the north side. And yes, an unfamiliar president occupied the ornate pedestal in front of the administration building, but there was nothing peculiar in this. The politics of San Mateo represented an unending struggle between the Bartolistas and the Recaldistas, complicated by the occasional intervention of the Phalangistas and the Communistas.

So the effigies of political heroes came and went on the Plaza. Only Bolivar had permanence, undisturbed by coups and revolutions, and the general populace seemed no more moved by the changes than the great Liberator himself. "Some day they will take up soccer," Julian used to say. "Then there will be real danger to life and limb."

All the same, it was no joke when you were questioned at the airport as a suspected purveyor of arms to the faction on the run.

Confound Julian! Whatever the trouble – flat tyre, choked carburettor, transmission – he should be here by now.

Lewis bought a paper from a newsboy and returned indoors. A heading on the front page posed a question in heavy type: "DO YOU WANT THEM BACK?" And the cutline under a double-column group picture was obviously in favour of a decided negative, for it identified the group as Enrique Bartol and his gang of bandits, taken at the last cabinet meeting before their overthrow.

Bartol himself seemed a jovial sort to Lewis, but perhaps the smile was merely a political trick. Some of his lieutenants were less prepossessing, and one or two of them looked as though the editorial description were justified.

The accompanying article talked of a new menace to the peace and prosperity of San Mateo. Exile had not damped the ardour of

Enriquito. The Bartolistas were plotting and the enemies of the Republic were aiding them. Eternal vigilance must be exercised. . . .

Insurrection, civil war! All the worn clichés were trotted out to titillate the clientele of the cafés but they left Lewis unmoved. He refused to be alarmed. All the years that Julian had lived in San Mateo he had been involved in only one political incident, and of that he had written in high glee.

Curiously enough, it had occurred at the time of Bartol's flight and one of the deposed ministers – one of those in the picture, no doubt – had figured in it, demanding hospitality at the point of a pistol and subsequently going to earth in a hole from which Julian had recently excavated a stone god.

Lewis scanned the group again, then turned the page. A long article on Juan Avila, San Mateo's distinguished composer, caught his eye. Lewis had never heard of Juan Avila, but Anne would probably be interested, so he tore the sheet carefully, folded the page, and stowed it in his wallet.

A few minutes later, deciding that it was useless to wait any longer for Julian, he telephoned the car-hire man recommended by Señor Balaguer.

CHAPTER VI

FROM THE FLOOR of the wide valley that dipped almost to sea-level at Trajano, there was a climb of nearly four thousand feet to the coffee country, but the goal could be reached only by traversing many miles of a road that was sometimes little better than a cart-track.

Under the most favourable conditions of weather by day it was a journey that took some four hours. Now there were storm clouds over the Cordilleras and night would fall before the worst part of the route could be passed.

Lewis expected resistance, protestations, arguments. How could anyone be expected to set out at this hour on such a drive? But the car-hire man took the order as if it meant no more than a run from the Cathedral to the Palacio Municipal. There was not even a whisper of *mañana,* and the fare, as fares went in San Mateo, was quite reasonable. Lewis was agreeably surprised. He suspected that the excellent Good Samaritan of the airport must have spoken in his favour.

Rain was falling in torrents when the car appeared, but the driver merely shrugged his broad shoulders. It was Lewis who thought of to-morrow, and only his anxiety to reach Julian made him resolute.

"It will not last," the driver said, but it lasted long enough to increase greatly the risks of the road.

The car forded swollen rivulets and slithered alarmingly over clay patches. The driver was an immovable torso behind the wheel.

He spoke once before the climb began. "This will take me longer than I thought. You will need to eat."

They stopped at a posada in the foothills. When they went on, the day was finished but the clouds had broken up, and mercifully, for the headlights were feeble, there was a moon.

The road dipped and soared in switchback loops, twisted on itself in hairpin bends, dived under hanging rocks, and swung along narrow ledges with precipitous falls. Then they were in the upland valleys, and the worst was over.

"This is Rosario," the driver said. "You will direct?"

Lewis tried to remember the way, but it was a long time ago. He leaned forward, peering ahead. Seeming familiarity of dim landscape was falsified by the next bend.

"I think . . ." He broke off. "Perhaps we had better inquire somewhere. Everyone knows the Casa Alta."

But the driver went on without hesitation, as if his question had been a mere formality.

A light gleamed through the black night of shady trees. Another mile, another light. Lewis made out the terraces of cultivated land. Then a road branched off to the eastward and that he thought must be the way to the little village of Rosario.

"We're quite close now," Lewis called. "On the left somewhere. You'll see a stone image at the beginning of the drive. Better slow down."

The driver slowed down a little. He reached for his switch and dipped his headlamps again and again.

"What's the matter?" Lewis asked, straining to see if there were anything on the road.

"It is the lights," the driver complained. "The battery is no good. I try to make better."

He found the stone image all right: a grotesque warrior gripping a mace as if to ward off intruders. The lights were strong enough now to show up the dead staring eyes, the flat nose, the lipless slit of the mouth, the indented cheek-bones.

Something moved behind the figure; a slinking animal, perhaps. The car turned into the driveway with no slackening of speed.

Now an avenue of evergreens led to a wide clearing, and Lewis saw the long low house with the hip-roof of grey tiles high-pitched above the single storey. Two short wings, new to him, partly enclosed a forecourt in which Julian had erected the grotesque trophies of his excavations. The fearsome gods and menacing warriors were a sinister crew in the moonlight, but, reassured by lighted windows, Lewis ignored them.

He was out of the car before the driver could move from his seat. He saw the familiar hall as the door was opened. He had words on his tongue to greet Pepe, the middle-aged houseboy, but the man who answered the bell was not Pepe, and, mingled with a queer embarrassment, Lewis felt a new misgiving.

Julian was not here. He had sold his Casa Alta and removed somewhere, in search of new gods.

The man in the entry stared at him with cold eyes in a dark face. Lewis stammered the name of his brother.

"You are Lewis Page, of course?" The man answered in English. "We have been expecting you. Unfortunately we had no one to send to the airport. Please to come in, Mr. Page."

"My brother is here?"

"Your brother is here. I am regretful that the news is bad for you. Don Julian is sick. Very sick. The doctor is with him now. You will forgive it if I am upset. I have been doing my best to look after things. Julian has mentioned me, perhaps? Benevides. Pascual Benevides."

"I don't recall." Lewis was dazed. He stared at the man for several seconds before he could frame the first of his questions.

Julian had been ill for many weeks. It had begun with some sort of fever, Benevides asserted. He was not acquainted with the jargon of the doctor, but, as he understood it, part of the cause – the fundamental weakening influence, in fact – was a recurrent malaria to which Julian was subject.

"I never knew of any malaria," Lewis asserted.

"No? Perhaps there are other things you never knew of. You must accept it now that your brother is dangerously ill. I am sorry if my words shock you, but I can see no purpose in hiding the truth. To be quite plain, I am most painfully anxious."

The hard set of the man's face and the cold indifference in his voice contradicted the claim.

Lewis continued to stare. In an emotional swirl of worry and alarm, there rose a quick eddy of dislike for Benevides. The man was a complete stranger to him, yet there was something puzzlingly familiar in his face. He was a neighbour, no doubt; another coffee-planter. Possibly he had been in the background ten years ago.

But Benevides, once encountered, was not a figure you were likely to forget. Everything about the heavy shouldered, thin-hipped body conveyed strength and latent agility, and the face added ruthlessness. The dark small eyes under level brows were intense with a sort of stony intensity, adder-like. The broad countenance, with the wide line of a thin-lipped mouth in near parallel to the brows, was that of the mountain Indian, but there was some evidence of a Spanish infusion, of alien blood filtered through the ages since the conquista. Certainly the narrow, well-shaped nose had come from Spain.

Lewis closed his eyes. Suddenly he was weak from an accumulation of weariness.

"I will go to Julian," he said. "I must talk to him at once."

"You shall go to him presently; but talk to him, no. Talking would do no good. He has been unconscious over many days. At the moment you will wait for the doctor. We will see what he will permit." The face was as hard as that of the stone image at the top of the drive. "Perhaps in the meantime, you will like to be shown to your room. I will see that a meal is prepared for you."

"Thank you. I have already eaten. I will stay here."

CHAPTER VII

THE DOCTOR was a small elderly man, nervous-looking, and a twitch that produced a hurt grimace was his only acknowledgment of Lewis. In contrast, he showed a deference towards Benevides that sometimes suggested a cringing. He spoke in Spanish, and Benevides translated. Lewis, rapidly recovering his own Spanish, could follow enough of the talk to realise that the interpretation was faithful.

"Your brother is dying, Mr. Page. The doctor says he has done everything possible, but the case has passed beyond the powers of medical science." There was something like an eagerness in Benevides to disclose all of the cruel substance. "This is the last stage of a disease that has wasted away the body, and the end may be only a matter of hours. Unfortunately there is little hope that he will regain consciousness. But, if you would like to see him, there is nothing –"

He broke off and jerked his head up alertly at a sudden sound from beyond the room.

It was the ringing of a telephone.

Bidding the doctor wait, Benevides hurried to answer the call. Lewis walked to the window and looked out. The broken, tumbled mass of the Cordilleras was bleak in the moonlight, but he saw nothing of it. He wanted to disbelieve what he had heard. It could not be true that Julian was dying. This old fool of a doctor was mistaken. An incompetent bungler. . . .

The doctor fussed with his bag, looking down as though afraid to meet the gaze of the Englishman.

At the telephone in the next room the voice of Benevides rose in anger.

"All the devils! What does she do with Maria Josefa? Why are my orders not obeyed? You will act at once. How long do you think we can wait?"

Lewis listened, translating the words automatically. The man was shouting in his rage.

"She should have been here hours ago. . . . Yes, yes, yes. At once! I do not care what time of night it is."

The receiver was smacked down violently on the cradle, and Benevides strode back into the room, his anger showing in his eyes.

"She has gone to the old hag," he snapped at the doctor. "That is why. You understand?"

"*Basta!*" The doctor's nervous reproof was accompanied by a slight gesture towards Lewis.

Benevides wheeled, his face expressionless again. "Mr. Page will pardon the interruption. It is my troublesome family."

"I don't understand." Lewis felt his dislike of the man growing.

"But there is nothing to understand." The voice undoubtedly had a sneer in it and the eyes were contemptuous.

"I am not concerned with your family." Lewis was suddenly indignant. "When I wished to telephone my brother from the airport, I was told that the line was out of order."

"To-day it was out of order. To-night it is working again. You wish to see your brother? I will ask Dr. Larreta to go with you. I think that will be best. You will be wise to control yourself when you enter. I will wait here, in case you have questions. The sick-room is too distressing for me. You will remember, please, that Julian is my dearest friend. Once he saved my life. That is why I do everything for him."

Passing from the full light of the living-room, Lewis could see little at first in the faint rose glow of a neon bulb at the side of the sick man's bed. An Indian woman rose from a chair, moved like a shadow, and halted before the doctor as if awaiting an order.

The air was heavy with the fragrance of flowers. Oleanders, perhaps; but no blooms were visible. There was something else, too; sickly, but faint. Lewis thought it was the seaweed smell of iodoform.

He felt Larreta's hand at his elbow, guiding him, and it seemed, at

27

the moment of contact, that the hand was shaking. He could make out the shape of a man under the coverlet; the darkness of a head against a pillow. When his eyes became used to the dim light, he could not believe that this man was his brother.

It was a corpse, he thought. Mummified.

He stared at the corpse. Then he saw the faint movement of breathing, and watched, scarcely breathing himself. There was no flesh on the face. The skin, blotched or shadowed, fell over the bones, and Lewis could see the pallor of it in the pink light of the low lamp.

"Julian!" He called the name loudly, losing control of himself in the agony of realisation.

The doctor's restraining hand was on him, but he threw it off fiercely.

"Julian! Julian!"

He stood by the bed, not daring to touch his brother for fear that he would end that feeble breathing. When at last he turned, the doctor was gone. The Indian woman, returned to her chair, was leaning forward, her eyes fixed on the bed. Her lips moved. A rosary hung in a loop from her hands, the little metal cross glinting as it swung in the neon glow.

Lewis went from the room in dismay, a sense of impotence upon him. He saw in the face of death a final frustration and he closed his eyes against the enormity of it. The guilt would be his if he allowed it to happen, but he felt he could do no more than the Indian woman with her rosary. Pray. . . .

Benevides was alone in the living-room, looking out through one of the windows, his back to the door.

Lewis saw again the familiar things that Julian had collected for his comfort, and his dismay turned to anger.

"Where is the doctor?" he demanded.

"By now he is on his way home." Benevides wheeled slowly. "He does not come to stay all night. He has many miles to go."

"Then send after him. Bring him back."

"One moment, Mr. Page." Benevides put a sorrowful note into it. "I can understand that you are upset, but there is no occasion for this excitement. Dr. Larreta has not spared himself in his service to Julian and I must insist on consideration for him. If you have questions to put, I will make the answers."

"Then tell me why Julian has been allowed to remain in this house. Why hasn't he been sent to a hospital in Trajano? He needs the best attention that can be given."

"What makes you think that he has not had the best of attention? What more do you imagine Trajano could do for him?"

"Are there no modern hospitals there? Bogota, then? It's no more than an hour or two by plane. If you are afraid to move him, I will take the responsibility."

"You are a specialist, perhaps, that you can diagnose his needs at a glance?"

"I can see that he is dying, and everything possible must be done."

"The first thing is to curb your own rash ideas, Mr. Page. How do you know what has or has not been done?" Benevides voice was sharp in protest. "Your brother remains in his own home by his own wish. More than a wish, it was a demand. Before he fell into this coma, his last word was an order. He refused to go to a hospital."

"A man so sick is not able to give such an order. How can you stand there and do nothing when you know he is dying?"

"Mr. Page, I try to make all allowances for you, but I am not going to listen to this sort of thing. Julian is in the hands of Dr. Larreta, and this again was his own wish. Dr. Larreta is an extremely competent man. None the less, he has not acted on his own judgment alone. I saw to it myself that he had the advice of the best minds in the country. We have had them here from Trajano for consultation, and they are in accord with Dr. Larreta entirely. They agree in one voice that nothing more can be done by the best hospital in the world. Julian is sick of an obscure tropical disease, and Dr. Larreta is the great specialist in that disease."

"I am not satisfied. I intend to call in a specialist myself. I will see that Julian is moved to the best clinic without delay."

"Is it to make trouble that you have come here?" The man's tone was quieter but more ominous. "Is it your wish to hasten your brother's death?"

"You need not worry yourself, señor." Dropping his voice in turn, Lewis put an icy edge on it. "Now that I am here you may consider your responsibility at an end."

"By what authority do you dictate to me?"

"Isn't the authority obvious?"

"The presumption is. You will remind me, of course, that you are Julian's brother. For myself, that is enough. I make no challenge. But there is another who has the duty to see that Julian's wishes are obeyed."

"I don't know what you're talking about."

"There seems to be quite a lot you do not know, Mr. Page. I am talking about the one who must have the final say. I am talking about Julian's wife."

"His wife!"

The words jerked from Lewis expressed but a small measure of his amazement. He stared at Benevides, disbelieving but confounded.

"His wife," Benevides repeated. "No doubt he would have written to you had he been able, but nothing here has gone normally. He became engaged to my sister four months ago. When he fell ill, he insisted on an immediate marriage."

"Your sister?"

"You seem to be shocked, Mr. Page, but I do not see why you should be. Julian and Leite were very much in love, and I think Julian realised that he would never recover from his illness. Naturally he wanted to make sure that Leite would inherit the estate, and she wished only to please him. It had to be arranged rather hastily — a civil marriage at the bedside — so there was no time to inform anyone."

Lewis heard only part of it as he struggled through incredulity to an acceptance of the probability. This, he had to admit, was just what the impulsive Julian might do. His whole history was made up of wild decisions, and, of course, he had reached a dangerous age when, as a bachelor, he might yield to allurement. Even a confirmed widower with a grown-up daughter could suddenly be set dreaming by the lovely face of a fellow-passenger on a plane.

"Are you listening to me, Mr. Page?" Benevides inquired. "I hope you are not too distressed."

"Where is your sister?" Lewis demanded. "I must speak to her."

Benevides shook his head. "Not at the moment. She was so worn out with nursing that the doctor sent her to bed. In the morning you will see her. Then you may be able to convince her that her husband should be moved."

CHAPTER VIII

THE POSITION was made quite clear. Whether Julian lived or died, Lewis had no authority of any sort in the household. Benevides was emphatic about that. His sister, he asserted, was quite solicitous that her husband's brother should be tendered every comfort, but Mr. Page must always remember that he was her guest – since Julian was incapable of acting as host – and it was hoped that as a guest he would respect the wishes of his hostess.

"I am ready to do so." Lewis tried to keep the bitterness out of his voice, but the antipathy he felt for Benevides must have been evident. "The sooner I meet your sister, the better," he asserted. "In the meantime, I shall wait by my brother."

"Do you mean to-night?" Benevides asked, with an inflection of pained surprise.

"Can there be any objection to that?"

"It is completely forbidden, Mr. Page." The tone seemed to convey regret. "Julian is carefully watched over at all times. You must have observed that he is in a very weak state. If, by any chance, he should recover consciousness, he would be quite unprepared for your presence, and we have been warned that even a small emotional disturbance could be disastrous. I do not want to believe, Mr. Page, that you have come here to cause us a new worry."

"Certainly not."

"Then you will permit yourself to be shown to your room. You are tired, I think, from your journey. After a rest, you will be in a better state for judgment."

Perhaps it was true. Perhaps weariness and anxiety were the springs of unjustifiable fears.

Lewis gave up and went to his room. He undressed and stretched out on the bed, but to rest was impossible. At best he could relax his body. The turmoil went on in his mind and was only increased by his efforts to resolve his bewilderment. He told himself that any woman that Julian had married must be a reasonable woman, a kind and gentle creature, yet he knew that the argument was absurd. Julian, like any other man, could be betrayed by his emotions. Like any other man . .

A cry that had a wild, inhuman note of agony in it caused him to start up. He listened in a sweat of fear. The sound was repeated, and then he knew that it was the wail of a night-bird. A guácharo, perhaps.

The cry came again, in the distance, echoing. There was a rustling, nearer, in the shrubbery outside. He rose and went to the window, but nothing was there that he could see. The scurrying sound of a small animal reached him. That was all.

He was lodged in the new east wing and his window looked out on the-forecourt with its gravelled drive and wide lawn and its stone images of gods and warriors deployed in two lines. They were, in Julian's words, the guardians of the house, but the Indians of the hills believed that they had power to bring misfortune to the man who had disturbed them.

Lights still burned in the main part of the house; in the hall, in the living-room. Lewis turned from the window, opened his door, and listened. The house was silent, and he had the thought that he might pass stealthily to Julian's room. A wish to see his brother again moved him, but he gave up the idea as soon as he had stepped through the doorway. Where the passage joined the corridor of the main house, an Indian servant sat, back to the wall, his legs sprawled out barring the way.

The man's head hung forward so that his chin was muffled in the folds of a short poncho. He might be asleep, but a movement close to him would surely wake him.

Benevides was making sure that Julian should not be disturbed.

Back in his room, Lewis paced in anger. In the morning there must be an end to this situation. In the morning he would insist on his authority whatever this wife of Julian's might say. He would go down to Trajano and demand the services of the best doctor he could find.

It was a programme. It was settled. He went back to bed, and then he began to think of Anne. First thing he would have to get a cable off to her. Whatever the preparations made, her voyage would have to be cancelled, for it was impossible to bring her here now.

Mentally he composed a message, amended it, made it more explanatory. Mentally he repeated it over and over, and some time in the process exhaustion overcame him and he dozed.

The sound of a car, the tyres grinding the loose gravel, brought him from his sleep. He struggled through a moment of fresh bewilderment, seeing unfamiliar objects in bright moonlight, hearing strange voices. Then he was alert, and anxiety returned like the pain of a wound.

A car in the night must mean that the doctor was here again, and that meant crisis. Julian . . .

He sprang from the bed and seized his dressing-gown. He heard voices in the forecourt and ran to the window. The car was standing in front of the main entrance, and the driver, a short, broad-built man, was opening the door for his passenger. Benevides came from the hall into the moonlight, and at that moment a woman emerged from the car.

A woman. Not the doctor.

The wave of the relief was like something tangible. Lewis gripped the window-sill.

Benevides spoke to the woman. The words were inaudible, but the tone expressed displeasure. He was protesting or complaining, and the woman retorted in a similar mood, her voice rising in pitch till Benevides cut in on her, caught at the sleeve of her loose coat, and turned her towards the house, obviously ordering her to get inside. Wrenching her arm from his grasp, she went quickly indoors. Benevides strode after her, and the driver followed with two suitcases and a small travelling bag.

Lewis waited. After a minute Benevides and the driver reappeared. They talked for a while earnestly, then parted. As the car rolled off along the drive, Benevides went back inside and closed the front door, and a moment later the lights in hall and living-room were switched off.

The time was seven minutes past four.

Lewis returned to his bed and settled himself once more. The house was a cage of silence in the still night, but not for long. The voices of Benevides and the woman were raised again in the main corridor, and next they were arguing hotly in a room that was either in or close to the east wing.

If they were man and wife, this was certainly no happy homecoming for Señora Benevides, but perhaps the husband had a reasonable cause for complaint in the hour of her arrival. Definitely he was putting his foot down, and shouting so that he could be heard all over the house.

"I'm giving the orders. You'll do as I command."

"No!" the woman cried. "You have no right."

Something crashed dully on the carpeted floor and a scream of pain made Lewis start for the door. The scream was cut off abruptly, as if by a smothering hand, and Lewis halted in the passage in a state of agonising indecision. The sounds he had heard suggested that murder might be done if no one intervened. Yet he was exaggerating, perhaps; putting a melodramatic construction on an episode that might mean little or nothing in the lives of jealous and hot-tempered people.

He hesitated and was spared. The slam of a door was like the shock of an explosion. Then the tread of a retreating male sounded from the corridor.

Lewis listened intently for fully a minute, but there was nothing more to hear.

At the end of the passage, the man in the poncho still sat on the floor with his legs sprawled out and his head bent forward.

CHAPTER IX

LEWIS AWOKE, startled by a knock on his door. He remembered dimly that he had seen the light of a dull dawn spread over the valley. Then he must have fallen asleep, and he had thought that he would never sleep. Now, in bright sunlight, he strove painfully to disentangle reality from the fantastic events of a nightmare.

The pain was actual. He had a monstrous headache. The knocking, too, was actual.

A servant opened the door and came in with a tray; a superior type of servant in a gleaming white mess jacket.

"Good morning, señor." He spoke in English with an American accent. "I have brought you some breakfast. Señor Benevides instructed that you were not to be called too early."

Lewis looked at his watch. Eleven! He threw back the bed-clothes as if he had heard a fire-alarm.

"There is no haste." The servant smiled affably. "When you have had your coffee, your bath will be ready. Señor Benevides sends his excuses. He is away on business till one o'clock. I am to report that the doctor has been and Don Julian is a little better. The Señora Page is sleeping late. The day is very beautiful, but here the morning is always quiet. There is no haste."

"What has become of Pepe?" Lewis asked.

"Pepe? I know no Pepe."

"He used to be the house-boy."

"I am the house-boy. My name is Manuel. The last one was a thief. Don Julian had to get rid of him. Maybe that was Pepe. If you want anything, you apply to me, please. The others speak no English. They

36

are ignorant mestizos."

Manuel was fastidious. The grimace that accompanied the reference to half-breeds stressed the high opinion he had of himself. Lewis wondered that Julian could tolerate the fellow after the lovable, devoted Pepe.

"The coffee is good," Manuel volunteered. "I made it myself." Then, as Lewis pulled on his dressing-gown and moved towards the door: "Where are you going, señor? The bath is not quite ready."

"Let me know when it is," Lewis snapped at him.

"Wait, señor, please. If you wish to see your brother, the doctor says it is possible. I will go with you."

The neon bulb still burned in the darkened room. A slight movement of the curtains in a current of air showed that the window behind them was open, but the atmosphere was still heavy with the oleander scent; heavy indeed, yet the same whiff of iodoform came through it. The day nurse, a younger Indian woman, stirred uneasily in her chair and focused sharp eyes on the intruder.

Lewis could see no change in Julian. He gazed down at the wasted, deathlike face and marked anxiously the feeble movement of breathing. He waited, watching for some variation, and at last he saw, or thought he saw, a feeble ripple of life under the skin.

"Julian!" He bent over the bed and called softly, his face close to the pillow.

The seaweed smell was stronger, puzzling. He associated iodoform with operations and surgical dressings. Possibly it might be used in the treatment of this obscure tropical disease. There could be some skin eruption, a rash.

"Julian! Can you hear me?"

The Indian woman started up nervously. The hovering Manuel protested.

"No. It is not allowed."

"Get out of my way." Lewis caught him off balance with a sudden push, then placed his hands gently on Julian's shoulders, vaguely hoping that the contact might rouse him.

"Julian!" His hands moved over the thin fabric of the pyjama jacket, feeling the emaciated body. Then, as the house-boy seized him and tugged at one arm, the jacket came open and he saw bandages.

Thrusting forward, the woman spoke to Manuel in an urgent mutter.

"She says you must go," he translated. "The doctor is very strict in his orders. Please, señor!"

"Take your hands off me!" Lewis pushed the fellow back again and the woman cried out wildly. Then the door was thrown open and Benevides strode in.

"So you are determined to make trouble, Mr. Page," he said. "If there is any more of it, you will force me to close this room to you."

The voice was cold and quiet. The menace was in the eyes of the man.

"What is the matter with my brother?" Lewis demanded. "Why is he bandaged? What are you trying to hide from me?"

"Hide? You are being absurd, my friend. It has been put to you very plainly that your brother is dangerously ill. All that concerns you is that he is getting the best of attention. He did not invite you here. He would be the first in deploring your behaviour. You have no rights in this house."

"Rights be damned! I want to know what is wrong with him."

"We will settle this matter at once. Your brother's wife is ready to see you. Come with me, and please try to calm yourself. You will realise, if you can, that my sister is going through a severe ordeal. She will expect to find sympathy from one so anxious about her husband."

Lewis somehow checked the desire to retort violently. Benevides wheeled abruptly and led the way to the living-room.

The woman was standing at the window with her back to the door, and Lewis saw the slender, well-formed figure almost in silhouette against the sunlight in the forecourt.

"My dear Leite," Benevides said. "I bring you Julian's brother."

She turned and came forward, and Lewis, made speechless by surprise, stared into the lovely troubled eyes that he thought were so beautiful. "Señora . ."

The word was formed and uttered somehow, and he continued to stare in incredulity.

She was the woman who had travelled on the plane from Cristobal to Santa Teresa.

CHAPTER X

THERE WAS NOTHING in her manner to suggest that a husband's brother meant anything to her. The frigid way in which she offered her hand – a formal tender under compulsion – might have implied that she was not interested in him or Julian.

When he was over the shock of the encounter, he began to think. Since she was Julian's wife, presumably in love with Julian, a little curiosity, even a little cordiality, might have been natural. Instead, she was remote, withdrawn, strange. She murmured a few words in Spanish. Then, as if recollecting herself, she added in English, mechanically, without any inflection: "I have heard so much about you from Julian."

Embarrassed by his puzzled gaze, she looked towards her brother. She was confused. Or shy. But there had been a moment when there was something like fear in her eyes.

"Mr. Page is very worried," Benevides said. "You must reassure him, Leite. I have confidence that he will believe you if you will tell him . ."

It was a long recital of what she should tell him; the familiar protest that everything possible was being done for Julian, but Lewis was not listening.

Benevides had claimed that his sister had retired early last night, worn out with nursing, and it was now obvious that the claim was false. She had not been in the house at the time. She was the woman who had arrived by car at four in the morning, and this was no mere surmise. The voice was evidence enough.

Lewis heard again the sounds of that quarrel in the night. He looked to see if there was any mark of violence on her, and at that moment she turned and met his gaze, and he saw, or imagined he saw, a plea in her eyes, as if she could read his mind.

His response was a stirring again of his resentment. She was part of some deception that was being practised upon him, and he could find no light of truth in the maze of his bewilderment. Julian's wife? Then she had left Julian in his illness. She had gone from San Mateo to Panama or beyond, and now she had been brought back to serve the purpose of Benevides. Because Julian was dying. . . .

"To put it plainly," Benevides was saying, "Mr. Page refuses to believe anything I say. You will tell him, Leite, that it is Julian's own wish that he shall not be removed from this house."

"That is so." The confirmation came in the expressionless voice.

"Then his wish should be overruled," Lewis answered harshly. "With your consent, señora, I will make arrangements at once."

"Tell him it is impossible, Leite."

"Let her speak for herself," Lewis shouted at the man.

"It is impossible," Leite said.

There had been hesitation, a moment of reluctance.

"The specialists forbid it," Benevides prompted her.

This time the echo was wanting. "You must settle it between you," she asserted with a flash of spirit. "I have nothing more to say."

"I have a lot more to say." Lewis stepped in front of her as she made a movement towards the door. "I want to know exactly what is wrong with my brother."

"Mr. Page is troubled by a little bandage." Benevides shrugged, and turned to address Lewis. "If you have patience to listen, I will explain. The sickness struck suddenly, while your brother was using a sharp pruning knife. In the collapse, he injured himself. Though not serious, the wound has been a little stubborn because of his poor physical state." He gestured, glancing towards his sister. "You were there when it happened, Leite."

The words were a command to her.

"I was there," she acquiesced.

Lewis followed it up sharply. "And you have been here all through his illness, nursing him?"

"I have told you that," Benevides intervened angrily. "Do you think I was lying?"

"Yes." Lewis was rigid, facing him. "Two days ago your sister travelled in the plane from Cristobal. I was on the same plane. I saw her leave Santa Teresa airport with the man who met her. I saw her arrive here by car at four this morning."

Leite's face was a blank. Only a nervous movement of her hands betrayed any feeling.

"A precise observer!" Benevides commented. "There are many tales to be told of mistaken identity. Some of them are even more strange."

"This time there is no mistake." Lewis shifted his focus. "Do you deny that you were on the plane, señora?"

"I . . . I think −"

"That's enough!" Benevides intervened again. "There is no need for an answer to such suspicions. You will listen to me, Mr. Page, and stop this persecution of my sister. Even if you were not mistaken, there is no law against a visit to Cristobal. If you saw her on a flight from Christmas Island, that would not make her any less the wife of your brother. It is true she was away for a while last night on a visit to an aunt. I was unaware of it until her return. Is that not so, Leite? You did go to see Maria Josefa without telling me?"

"I should have taken her advice." The answer in Spanish came with a tone of desperation. "I wish to hear no more."

She moved towards the door, but Benevides grasped her by one arm and pulled her back.

"Wait!" he shouted. "And speak in English, or there will be more baseless suspicion. I have been very patient with your brother-in-law, but I will take no more from him. We know why he is here. We know that the hatred he shows for us comes from his own disappointment."

He faced Lewis menacingly.

"It was a shock to you, Julian's marriage, wasn't it? You imagined you had only to show yourself here to get anything you wanted. I saw your cables asking for money. Julian was too sick to deal with them, or you would have had a quick refusal. Since his marriage it has been his one purpose to protect his wife's interests. His estate is tied up. He is no longer in a position to make extravagant gifts. And it will be well for you to understand that you will gain nothing by his death, if that is what you are hoping for."

"You'll know what I'm hoping for when he's out of your hands." Lewis was shaking with anger. "Get out of my way!"

"Why?" Benevides moved to cover the door. "Am I in your way? What do you think you are going to do?"

"I'm going to see that my brother is placed under proper care. At once."

"Still meditating on specialists and clinics? I advise you to forget them, Mr. Page. I am in charge here, and I will have no interference from you."

"We'll see about that when I reach Trajano. I'm beginning to think that this is a case for the police."

"No, no!"

The protest came from Leite. Lewis saw her strained face, and now he was in no doubt of the fear in her eyes.

Benevides said: "How do you imagine you are going to get to Trajano?"

Lewis knew that there was a garage at the first road junction. If he failed to hire a car, he would walk.

"I'll find a way," he retorted. "Don't you worry about that."

"I am not worrying. Not at all, Mr. Page. Not at all." Benevides moved back a step, but he was still covering the door. "I am not worrying because you are not going to Trajano."

"How are you going to prevent me?"

"This way." With a swift movement of his right hand, Benevides pulled a revolver from his jacket pocket. "Now stop being foolish, Mr. Page. Sit down and relax."

CHAPTER XI

BENEVIDES REGRETTED exceedingly that he had been forced to make a demonstration of armed strength, but he knew about those specialists in Trajano. They were always in conflict, and he was going to take very good care that Julian was not made a victim of their whims and prejudices. If Mr. Page would only see reason, he need suffer no discomfort.

Lewis could see only that he was a prisoner. He was allowed a certain freedom in the house and on the estate, but he was quickly to discover that, wherever he went, a shadow was not far away.

Since his arrival he had been concerned only for Julian, and Julian was still his prime worry, but after the scene with Benevides he began to think of his own predicament too. He had come with little money and it might be a long time before he could expect any help from Julian. A long time, or never. If Julian died, he would have to draw on the slender resources left in his business to get back to London. Either that, or borrow from Anne's untouched legacy from her mother.

Anne!

He swore at himself bitterly. The cable he had rehearsed in the night had been forgotten in the disturbances of the morning. He blamed himself for oversleeping. He called himself an impetuous fool for his decision to bring her out here. The need to stop her was more than ever urgent.

A spare cable-form was in his wallet and on the back of it he found the telephone number of the company's office in Trajano. No one interfered with him when he lifted the receiver from the instrument in the hall, but the line was dead.

Manuel appeared suddenly, grinning. "The extension is disconnected, señor," he said. "You will have to go to the office."

Benevides was in the office.

"It is a pity to deny your daughter such a happy voyage, but I understand your dilemma." Benevides was amused. "There is no need to telephone. If you will write your cable, I will see to it personally. I am driving in to Trajano at once. Do not look so doubtful at me, Mr. Page. Your reason should tell you that I am not anxious to have another impediment in this house."

"I prefer to use the telephone, if you don't mind."

"I prefer not." Benevides changed his tone. "Write your cable, if you desire it to be sent."

Lewis wrote. Benevides read the message. "It should be more imperative, but it will do," he commented. "If there is anything you wish from Trajano, I am at your service."

"How long to you propose to keep me prisoner?"

"Do you so regard yourself?" Benevides had put on a pair of dark glasses, and, with the quick malignancy of his eyes blanked out by the large black-gleaming goggles, he seemed older and almost benign. "You have forced me to restrain you from an act that would be quite opposed to your brother's wishes. That is all, Mr. Page. I know you are unwilling to leave your brother while he is gravely ill, and my sister appreciates this. She wants you to feel you are a welcome guest until there is a change. In the circumstances, I am sure you will do nothing to cause her further embarrassment."

The grin, without the eyes to give it sardonic point, might have passed for affable. Lewis almost expected an appeal to let bygones be bygones. Instead, clapping a loose and rather worn panama on his head, Benevides said: "Be careful which way you walk, Mr. Page."

Lewis was alone at lunch. Doña Leite, Manuel explained, had a slight indisposition. She wished to be excused.

"It is a very beautiful afternoon for a promenade," Manuel suggested. "If you wish, señor, I will show you the way along the valley."

"Thank you. I remember the way."

45

"But it is not wise to go into the jungle. There are bad snakes. Very poisonous."

"Why should I go into the jungle?"

"Exactly, señor. It is a good place to keep out of. My brother did not think so. He was bitten. Dr. Larreta saved his life. He injected here." Manual pointed to his stomach. "Very good doctor. The best doctor in San Mateo. My brother was very lucky."

"What you want me to believe is that *my* brother is very lucky?"

Manuel sighed. "Poor Don Julian! When he married he was so very happy. And now . . ." He shrugged sadly, then beamed. "Dr. Larreta will be here again to-night. Every day he comes twice, sometimes three times."

The fellow might be genuine. For a set piece of garrulity it sounded almost too disingenuous. Lewis fired in a sudden question.

"Why did Doña Leite go to Cristobal?"

"Cristobal?" Manuel went on pouring a cup of coffee. "When was that, señor? She has been here always. She would never leave Don Julian. She is with him night and day. You wish it white, señor?"

"Black."

When he went to the sick-room there was no interference. The Indian woman offered him a chair, and he stayed a while, sharing her watch. He wondered when the devoted wife would come, but was left to go on wondering. There was still no change in Julian, no sign that he would ever come back to the life he had enjoyed so well.

Perhaps by to-night Dr. Larreta would find some change.

Lewis was oppressed by his own impotence. He could do no good sitting here, staring at the sick man while the Indian woman stared at him. He got up and walked out into the sunlight and the glare of it set him blinking. He saw Manuel watching from the veranda of the main house, and he had an impulse to see how far he might be permitted to wander.

He was stopped at the end of the drive by an alert young man in denim slacks and a sort of wind-cheater. When he tried to push past into the highway, the young man's right hand dived into the wind-cheater and for the second time that day Lewis saw a menacing revolver. About to expostulate, he checked himself. It seemed that everyone believed that he was ignorant of Spanish, and it might be as well if they went on believing it.

The sentry shouted at him and gestured wildly in the direction of the house.

"*Vuelvese !*" he shouted. "*Vuelvese !*"

Lewis shrugged and went back.

Out of sight round the first bend in the drive, he might have turned into the bordering shrubbery and found a way to the road unseen, but he knew he would not get far along the road before he was intercepted. Benevides was not one to leave open such a loophole.

Lewis returned to the forecourt and continued past the house, taking the path along the side of the steep valley that was roughly terraced and planted with coffee under the shade of guamo trees. He saw that Manuel was still watching from the veranda, but no one followed him. This way he might stray at will for there was no exit that he would dare to use; only the sheer cliff of a ravine and the tangle of jungle that spread over the hills.

The coffee berries shone red and cherry-like through the glossy dark green of the oval leaves. On his previous visit to the Casa Alta he had seen the natives, both men and women, swarming along the valley with their wide, bowl-shaped baskets, selecting and gathering the ripe "cherries," but now no pickers were at work. The whole plantation seemed deserted, and a good crop was wasting away.

He went on and on along the winding valley, but long before he came to the fringe of the jungle he turned and walked slowly back to the house. On the gravel of the drive stood a shining new American car, and a liveried chauffeur lounged in the shade of the nearest stone god, reading a newspaper.

Indoors Lewis encountered Manuel hurrying along the corridor with a tray. Manuel looked worried, but stopped and produced a sudden beaming smile.

"You had a nice walk, señor, yes?"

Lewis ignored the question.

"Is the doctor here? Is that his car?"

"No, no. It belongs to Doña Maria Josefa." Manuel's worried look came back. "I have just taken maté to the solana. I think Doña Leite expects you. Will you come, please?"

Maria Josefa! Evidently a lady of consequence. Lewis remembered the name. The old hag of Benevides's aside to Dr. Larreta.

It was obvious that Doña Leite was not expecting him. She was embarrassed when Manuel brought him to the sun-parlour where she and her guest were sipping maté through silver bombillas. She introduced Lewis with quickly affected graciousness, describing the guest as her aunt, Señora Mayorga.

Maria Josefa was a grim-faced, elderly woman with blue-tinted white hair, a sharp eagle nose, and small, darting black eyes. She acknowledged Lewis's bow with a mechanical smile, then turned to the hostess and delivered a vituperative comment in a level, expressionless voice.

"Some day I will take a horsewhip to that Manuel. I am not welcome here, so he interferes by bringing in this foreigner."

"I can do nothing about it," Doña Leite replied, glancing nervously at Lewis.

Maria Josefa had no doubts about the foreigner's reputed ignorance of Spanish. "You can come away with me now, Leite," she urged. "Before it is too late."

"No. I have to think of Enrique."

"A fool! A fool of fools! He will get nowhere with such a clique."

"Please . ."

Maria Josefa turned back to the blank-faced Lewis with another fleeting mechanical smile.

"Pardon, señor," she said. "It is rude that we talk in Spanish, but my English is not good. I was asking about you. So it is that you are the brother of our Don Julian?"

Leite intervened. "Will you drink maté, Mr. Page?"

Maria Josefa cackled grimly. "Do you address your brother-in-law so formally? But, of course, you are scarcely acquainted. Certainly he will not drink maté. I never knew an Englishman who would give up his tea for the *yerba buena*. Order some Darjeeling, Leite."

Lewis observed that her English was far from bad. He said: "You are kind, madame, but to-day I prefer maté. I have learned to appreciate it."

"I understand that Don Lewis has been in San Mateo before."

There may have been a warning note in Leite's remark. Maria Josefa developed a qualm.

"You speak Spanish, señor?"

"My business leaves me little time for language study." Lewis put regret into his voice and Maria Josefa was reassured. She talked. She was almost as garrulous as the detested Manuel, but it was idle talk, and when she lapsed into Spanish she always translated the terms for Lewis, except when she rose to depart. Then Lewis had to translate for himself.

"I must go before your precious half-brother gets back," she asserted.

Half-brother! Involuntarily Lewis turned to stare at Leite. The term explained the lack of resemblance.

"I don't know when he will return," Leite answered.

"Perhaps never. Does the imbecile think no one will ever recognise him in those insane goggles?" She gathered her belongings. "Poor Enrique! Between you all, he will end up with his back to a wall."

Tall and lean and hawk-like, she swivelled towards Lewis. "Again your pardon, señor," she said. "Come, Leite! You will see me to the car. Your brother-in-law will excuse us."

Her heels and the ferrule of her stick clicked on the tiled floor of the sun-parlour. She walked stiffly, like an ill-made puppet, and her head nodded with every step. She was very old.

Left alone, Lewis looked out from one of the great windows that Julian had designed. Far away the snow capped cone of a dead volcano gleamed among the lesser Andean peaks, but he saw nothing of the extravagant panorama. He was trying to put the bits and pieces together. A word, a sentence, a name – but there was no key to it that he could find.

Leite came back to retrieve a forgotten handbag.

"I am sorry for what happened this morning," she said. "Pascual is sometimes hot-tempered. When he has made up his mind, he will not be crossed."

"Why do you say this to me?" Lewis asked coldly. "Are you not with him in what he is doing? I am made a prisoner in my brother's house. In your house. Is that your wish? It is not Julian's."

She met his gaze for a moment. Then faltering, she turned quickly and left him.

CHAPTER XII

AT DUSK a group of men came along the valley path from the coffee terraces. They were followed by others in twos or threes and they all assembled at the far end of the forecourt, away from the house. Fifteen. Lewis counted them.

They wore rough, earth-stained labouring clothes. Some had thrown ponchos over their shoulders against the chill of the coming night, but none of them was like the natives of the Rosario district who normally picked the coffee berries. They were tall, strong fellows, different from the broad-built, big-lunged mountain men.

Lewis wondered. He had seen the type on the wharves of Santa Teresa. They might be stone-masons, builders, tough hands from the river steamers that made the tortuous way along the Medina between Trajano and the Pacific coast. Anyway, they were not coffee-pickers, for no one had gathered the red berries that day.

They lounged on the edge of the lawn, some of them resting their backs against one of the stone images. They smoked cigarettes, and the murmur of their voices reached the house. One of them sang a tired song in a nasal tenor. Manuel went out to them and they rose and stood at attention as if he were someone important. When he returned, they relaxed again, waiting.

Then, while there was still a little light in the sky, an open truck drove in from the roadway, backed and turned. The workers lined up and climbed on board, the driver switched on his head lights, and started off.

Lewis listened to the diminishing sound of the engine. A moment later he heard it whining in low gear as the truck climbed the steep gradient behind the house. The direction was away from Trajano. The men were being taken up into the wild highlands of the border country.

For quite a while the sound of the engine was audible. When it was finally lost in the distance the gods and warriors in the forecourt were vague black shapes in the night.

In the morning the truck brought the men back again, and they trudged off along the valley side. Perhaps Julian had given orders for more excavations and Benevides was seeing that the work was carried on. But it had always been a principle with Julian to employ the mountain men.

Lewis questioned Manuel. "They are hired to work," the houseboy answered. "That is all I know. It is none of my business. There is always some work to be done."

"There's work here that is not done. Where are the coffee-pickers?"

"I am not the manager of this finca. The pickers will come some time. It is likely that your brother is not worrying. Why should you be?"

Instead of his usual mocking politeness, Manuel had assumed the truculent authority of a Benevides. The household was upset, and this might be the cause of the change. Benevides had not returned from Trajano. In a brief glimpse he had had of Leite, Lewis had seen that she was very worried, and he recalled Maria Josefa's scathing remark about the goggle-wearer.

Leite's anxiety pointed up the significance of it. Someone might recognise Benevides in spite of the dark glasses!

It was now nine o'clock and apparently nothing had been heard of him.

Leite, coming to breakfast, greeted Lewis with grave formality and at once spoke to Manuel.

"Did he say that he might be away all night?"

"No." Manuel's tone was as anxious as her own. "He expected to be back before midnight."

"You'd better telephone Mauricio."

"I have. They parted at eight. He is to call back at once if he hears anything."

"What are you going to do?" She appealed to Manuel as if he were now in charge.

"Nothing," he answered. "Nothing can be done till we have news."

Leite turned to Lewis. "Forgive me, please. My brother is such a reckless driver and the road is not of the best."

Lewis was inclined to express the hope that he had broken his neck. What he said was: "I trust nothing has happened to him."

Manuel brought her toast and coffee. This time she spoke to him in English.

"Have you been for the mail?"

"I will drive down now, if you will excuse me, madame." Manuel was the correct houseboy again.

Lewis said: "I'm expecting a cable from my daughter. Will it be delivered to the house?"

"Yes, sir. It will be telephoned to the local post office from Trajano. A messenger will bring it out."

"The office is two kilometres from here," Leite explained. "Telegrams are delivered, but the mail has to be collected."

"Perhaps Manuel will post an air-letter for me?"

Manuel declined. "I am sorry. You will have to ask Don Pascual."

"But he is not here. The letter is merely to my daughter in London."

"I am sorry, señor."

So there were to be no letters, except by favour of Benevides. Anne would have to wait for a full explanation of the cable cancelling her trip.

Julian was still in his coma, but Dr. Larreta, on his morning visit, expressed himself more hopefully. Perhaps by the night there would be a favourable turn.

Lewis walked along the valley again and this time went to the end of the coffee trees and halted at the beginning of the jungle path. He remembered how the path climbed steeply through the tangle to the high terrace where Julian had unearthed most of his gods. He remembered the fork that led to the place where the largest image had been excavated, the wide track cut through the dense growth so that the immense mass of stone could be trundled out to the clearing.

If there were new excavations in progress, the terrace would be the likely spot, and certainly it seemed that the path was being used.

Lewis advanced a few yards into the jungle, peering with the intensity of a tracker at the trampled surface of the narrow way. The stub of a cigarette was a sufficient sign that someone had been there quite recently, and he pushed on up the ascending cat-walk, brushed by the leaves of spindly saplings and the outflung fronds of ferns.

At the point where the path divided a man rose from a fallen tree-trunk to bar his way. Lewis was not surprised. Neither was the sentry. He held up a large forbidding hand in the manner of a policeman on point duty and shook his head. He smiled. He was a big, handsome lad with frank eyes.

Lewis pointed up the path to the terrace.

"No." The sentry shook his head again.

Lewis shrugged and turned back. He had learned that the ascending way was overgrown. It had not been used for some time. But the track that forked off to the left through a stretch of level jungle was clear and much trampled.

Round the first bend on his retreat Lewis paused and listened. He could not have been more than fifty yards from the point where the solitary god had been found, but he heard nothing to indicate that work was in hand at that place; no talk, no thud of picks or rasp of shovels. The workers, he was sure, had gone that way, but the jungle had swallowed them and the jungle was being secretive about it. There was silence except for the chatter of birds.

When he reached the house, relaxed tension told him that Benevides had returned. Manuel was cheerful again, ready to be loquacious, and at lunch Leite tried to be friendly in an evidently genuine attempt to ease his situation. Now he found in her the quality that his imagination had given her on the plane trip from Cristobal. She might, in his view, be allied with her half-brother against him, but she was fundamentally warm-hearted. She saw how worried he was and wished to relieve him, yet when he spoke of Julian she was singularly detached and evasive, answering at second-hand. The doctor had said so-and-so, or her brother thought. . .

"You should have been spared all this," she said, "but no one believed you would come all the way from England. Certainly Pascual would have warned you about Julian's illness. He was very disturbed when your telegram arrived from Santa Teresa."

"If I had heard of the illness, I would have come sooner." Lewis watched her closely. "I can't understand why I was not told of your marriage."

"We decided rather suddenly." She looked down at the table.

"Had you known each other very long?"

"Not . . ." She hesitated. Or she seemed to catch her breath. "Not very long."

She raised her head and he saw tears in her eyes. She had seemed so remote from Julian when speaking of him that this sudden emotion surprised and moved him.

"I'm sorry," he said.

"Sorry?" She shrugged off the tears as if ashamed of them. "You have no occasion to be sorry for me."

A curious creature. There was something like defiance in the still tearful eyes that met his solicitous gaze.

"I think it is I who must be sorry," she added, and in the same breath asked him: "Did you get the cable you were expecting?"

"Not yet."

"You are worried. It is something important?"

"Didn't your brother tell you?"

She was puzzled. "What has my brother to do with it?"

Lewis explained. Naturally, he said, he was anxious to have an assurance that his daughter had cancelled her trip.

"She may have replied by night letter," Leite suggested. "It should be delivered with the mail to-morrow morning."

This was possible, he thought, and he continued to think so, but nothing came with the mail in the morning. Anne was sometimes negligent, a little irresponsible in practical matters, yet he had asked her to reply without delay.

All the day he remained in the house, hoping for a messenger from the local post office. Benevides had followed the workers along the valley and was away till late in the afternoon. Doña Leite, Manuel announced, was keeping to her room, worn out again.

The only caller was the doctor, and this time he discussed his patient with Lewis in fluent English. Again the signs were favourable. The pulse was more regular, the breathing easier.

"Once we disperse the coma, there should be an improvement. Then, with normal feeding, the recovery should be rapid. But I must warn you, señor, that you may find the mental attitude changed, the sort of change that is sometimes the sequel to encephalitis lethargica."

"Is that what it is?" Lewis asked hastily.

"There were symptoms of it in the early stage, following the first acute attack of malaria. We have here, in San Mateo, a leading authority on sleeping sickness. I have consulted him, but we were unable to reach a definite conclusion."

Dr. Larreta blinked and looked away. "If I tell you that I, myself, am recognised as an authority on tropical diseases, you will understand that it is with the wish to reassure you. I have given many years to research in these diseases, particularly malaria. That is why señor Benevides insists that I remain in charge of the case."

"How long has my brother been in this coma?"

"Since one day before your arrival. Previously there were periods of stupor and some delirium. But to-day I am encouraged. Perhaps we are now at the turning point."

Dr. Larreta relaxed and smiled. "You are in good health yourself, Mr. Page. That I can see. But beware of our climate. The sudden changes at this altitude are sometimes dangerous to the stranger." He picked up his worn visiting-bag and turned towards his car. "Well, my friend, if anything goes wrong, send for me at once."

Lewis said: "Will you post a letter for me, please?"

"I would be happy, but I do not go that way. You should ask Manuel."

Once more the slam of the prison gate.

Lewis watched the elderly Buick receding down the drive. It seemed to him then that Larreta had treated him like the inmate of an insane asylum, humouring him with a lot of talk that might not mean a thing. Unless it had been designed to allay suspicion.

In the evening Benevides joined his sister and Lewis at the dining-table. He was in high spirits. He joked with Manuel, attended Leite with a show of affection, and was mockingly affable towards Lewis.

"The best wine in the house, Manuel," he ordered. "To-night we celebrate."

Leite was unresponsive. "What do we celebrate?" she asked sombrely.

"Discovery. We have success at last. Everything is turning out as I foresaw."

He had been with the workers all day, but it was not possible that he could be so elated over the finding of another stone image. Unless he was another fanatic, like Julian.

For a moment a look in Leite's eyes suggested that she, too, might have her fanaticism. The puzzled Lewis observed a succession of emotions in her. Relief followed triumph, but more he could not define.

She exclaimed rapidly in Spanish and all Lewis could catch was a suggestion that now things would be different.

The more deliberate reply of Benevides was easier to follow. "There will be no change. We go on as we have arranged."

"I will talk to you later."

"There is nothing to talk about." Benevides frowned.

"Later!" She looked to Lewis as a means of changing the subject. "Did you hear from your daughter, Mr. Page?"

"No." Anxiety was immediately uppermost again. "Perhaps to-morrow."

"But there has been time." She turned to Benevides. "Pascual, did you send that cablegram for Mr. Page?"

"What cablegram?" Pascual asked good-humouredly.

Lewis jerked his head back. "The one I gave you two days ago," he said protestingly.

"I have no recollection of any cablegram."

"You were starting for Trajano." Lewis shouted in sudden anger.

"You promised to send it for me."

"Trajano?" Benevides affected bewilderment. "I was very busy that day. I must have forgotten. No doubt it is still in my pocket. Was it very important?"

"You know how important it was." Leite stared at him coldly. "If the girl is now on the way, it is through your fault."

"My fault?" Benevides put indignation into it.

"What has it to do with me if Mr. Page wants to bring his daughter to San Mateo? She has not cabled that she is coming. Perhaps she has decided for herself to stay at home."

"I have warned you, Pascual. I . . ."

"Keep quiet!" An ominous leap in his voice was accompanied by the thud of his fist on the table.

"You will not talk to me like that." Her own voice was cold and hard. "I have warned you how far I will go."

"All the devils! What is this girl to you? If she comes, she will be looked after. You shall have the ordering of it. She will be happy to make the acquaintance of her new aunt, no doubt. That is enough."

"Why did you not send the cable?"

"Enough!" His fist crashed on the table again. "Manuel!" he shouted. "Where is that wine?"

Lewis got up and walked from the room.

CHAPTER XIII

HE HAD TO BREAK out of this place, seek advice, establish his authority as Julian's brother. He could no longer accept the situation merely because he wished to remain close to the sick man. Neither could he wait patiently for Julian to recover. And he was not to be deterred by a flourishing of pistols. Melodramatic gestures were native to these people, part of their quarrelsome temperaments, their sudden excitability. They were gestures that meant no more than schoolboy threats of mayhem and neck-breaking. The idea that anyone might pull a trigger was preposterous.

Even if escape entailed walking all the way to Trajano, he would accomplish it somehow. He would see the British Consul and explain everything to him. But the case, if he went beyond the facts, was a little difficult to explain, and the facts were very simple. His interference had been resented, he had been threatened and placed under restraint.

"Of course," the Consul would say, "I sympathise with you, Mr. Page, but it is natural for these people to safeguard your brother, even by extreme means, if they are convinced that their doctor is the right man."

"But don't you see that there's something strange going on?"

"In what way, Mr. Page?"

"Well, this doctor, for instance –"

"But Dr. Larreta is a distinguished man, an acknowledged expert on tropical diseases."

"Take the woman, then. She was on that plane from Cristobal."

"Mr. Page! Cristobal is a few hours away by air. In this country people use planes as we at home use buses."

"Then why not tell the truth about it? Why all these evasions and prevarications?"

"Why should anyone confide in an intruder? That is what you are, sir. An intruder. These people are trying to save your brother's life. What do you want me to do about them? Call the police? Have them arrested?"

"The doctor –"

Always, in the cycle of that imaginary interview, he came back to Larreta.

"What about this talk of a changed mental attitude, the sort of thing that follows sleeping sickness? Wasn't he preparing me for some form of deterioration?"

"My dear sir, are you suggesting that this is a case of brain-washing?"

"Exactly. He's giving my brother injections. What sort of injections? Drugs can condition the brain to anything. To an unwished marriage, let us say; to the acceptance of an unwanted wife."

"Dear, dear! Always harping on the woman! If she is as attractive as you say, would it require a shot in the arm to make her seem desirable? I think, Mr. Page, you have been reading some pseudo-scientific horror stories."

"Then there's nothing you can do for me?"

"Not as British Consul. As a private individual, I can give you the address of a good psychiatrist."

The anguished Lewis looked out upon the dark shadows of the gods in the forecourt. In the dining-room behind him, the two he had left were shouting at one another, wolf and wildcat again.

This was something that the smug, complacent Consul should hear. Then he would believe that there was justification for a complaint.

"Justification, Mr. Page? Merely a matter of temperament. These Latin-Americans, you know! Probably the altitude!"

Lewis went into the living-room and searched the book-case till he found an old medical encyclopaedia.

"Coma is a condition of. . ."

He knew what coma was.

"It may result from the effect of poisons on the nervous system . . . alcohol . . . opium . . . the derivatives from barbituric acid . . . malaria, sleeping sickness, diabetes . . . coma vigil . . . severe fevers . . ."

Larreta might have spoken by the book.

From the article on encephalitis lethargica Lewis learned little more than the doctor had told him.

But none of this need necessarily apply to the case of Julian. Larreta had invoked it merely to plant an idea in the mind of his interlocutor. It was he, Lewis, who was being brain-washed.

He returned the book to the shelf and walked out on to the veranda. He was finished with the imaginary Consul. There was not a shred of evidence that he could lay before anybody. Peculiar acts and reactions; a few things overheard and perhaps misconstrued, for his Spanish was faulty; and he had nothing more but suspicion.

The game they were playing might be a conspiracy to put him out of his brother's favour, and, if this were all, Julian would soon resolve it. Just as soon as he recovered consciousness. . . .

Larreta's car materialised out of the night. Lewis waited, but he had no opportunity of talking to the doctor when he came from the sick-room. Benevides did all the talking, and Benevides had brought his anger from the dining-room. Larreta was a diminished creature, spluttering nervously, protesting feebly about something.

Lewis could catch no word of what was said. He could gather only that Benevides was dissatisfied with Larreta, but no comfort was to be derived from this. All he now had was the hope that the turning point in Julian's illness was really near.

When the house was quiet he went to the sick-room. The Indian women were used to his visits by now and took no notice of him. One of them was always there, seated in the chair, telling a rosary or straining at needlework in the faint glow from the neon bulb.

To-night there was another visitor. Leite stood by the bed, motionless, staring down at Julian. Perhaps she came often, but this was the first time that Lewis had seen her there. He closed the door silently and waited. For a long time she held that rigid pose; so long a time that his eyes became accustomed to the half light.

At last she moved back a step. Her shoulders lifted and her elbows jerked to her body in a shudder. She turned, and he saw her face clearly in the rose glow. There was something like hatred in her look, or it might have been disgust. Disgust with sickness, perhaps; with the wasted, corpse-like figure it had made of a man.

When she saw Lewis her face became blank, and she passed without a word or a second glance at him.

He moved hopefully towards the bed, but he could find not the slightest sign of improvement in Julian, and after his period of watching he went away with the conviction that Larreta had deceived him.

The night for him was troubled by anxiety and despair, yet in the morning hope returned. The doctor himself might be wrong, if he had lied. Some time the coma had to end.

Lewis was alone at breakfast. Benevides had already gone off along the valley on the trail of the labourers. Manuel supplied that much information, but, pressed for more, he was silent and surly. He had become less and less talkative, more and more insolent.

"You can help yourself to coffee," he said. "I have to attend to Doña Leite."

"Have you been for the mail?"

"There is nothing for you."

But surely Anne must have sent some reply to his message from Santa Teresa. Benevides was holding it back. Or there had been some hitch, some delay in arranging her passage.

He was cheered by the hope that she was still safe in London, but it did not survive the moment.

On his way to the sick-room he saw that Manuel was at work in the office. Only Manuel was allowed to clean the office. The precious telephone had to be guarded, by lock or the faithful houseboy. No extension could be used without the permission of Benevides. But the telephone was something that Lewis had come to ignore. There was no one to whom he could appeal.

The watching Indian woman gave him a word of greeting and moved a chair for him. He sat close to the bed. This time he intended to share the watch till the doctor came. Then he would insist on staying, so that he might see what went on.

He leaned forward in his chair and spoke, as he always did.

"Julian, old man! Can't you hear me?"

The Indian woman took no notice. She was used to these vain conjurations of the foreigner.

He saw, or imagined he saw, a faint trembling of the nostrils, but he had deceived himself many times. It was some effect of the feeble breathing, or it might be an illusion caused by waves of vibration from the vacuum cleaner in the office.

The vacuum-cleaner whined so loudly, he had to lean farther forward to listen to the breathing.

He thought the low sound of a sigh must be more self-deception, yet it had seemed so real that it drew from him a sharp whisper of appeal.

The Indian woman, at her morning devotions, was in a trance of prayer, her fingers moving from bead to bead.

"Julian!"

This time there could be no mistake about the response. Lewis heard the rasping respiration and saw a movement under the skin of the throat.

Julian opened his eyes, closed them, opened them again. Tensely, Lewis bent nearer.

"Lewis . . ." The name was scarcely audible. The lips continued to move, and Lewis was silent, holding his breath for fear he might miss a word.

"Where's Anne? Did you bring . . . ?"

Julian's eyes closed, and the watcher had the fear that the coma had taken him away again.

"She's coming, old boy. She's on the way. We'll meet her together at Santa Teresa."

The Indian woman looked up from her beads and crossed herself, but was unaware of anything unusual.

She lowered her eyes and began another decade of Aves.

"Julian! You're all right now. Do you hear what I say? You'll soon be on your feet again."

"No."

By a convulsive effort Julian lifted his head from the pillow. Lewis held him, and his hands reaching behind the thin shoulders felt the trembling of the body. The thin voice rose to a cry, and the Indian woman was on her feet, staring, unable to believe what she saw.

"Lewis!" Julian cried. "Keep them away. They're killing me. They want . . . want . . . want . . . Oh, God!"

He was in agony, trying to get his breath. Then the woman believed, and she ran from the room, screaming shrilly for Manuel, for Doña Leite, for anyone who would come.

The whine of the vacuum-cleaner died in a complaining moan, but there was a new noise to accompany the clamour in the corridor: the swish of tyres on gravel outside the window. The doctor had arrived.

Lewis heard nothing but the frantic voice of his brother.

"The drugs ... It began . . . began . . . Izar-izarzar-zar-br-br . . ."

The meaningless sounds were forced out between chattering teeth. Julian struggled and another word emerged.

"Poison, poison, poison . . ."

He kept on repeating it as though the mind, beaten by the shivering body, could go no farther.

Hands from behind seized Lewis and he was sent staggering back from the bed till the door-post saved him from falling. Manuel was there, shouting Spanish oaths, reaching out as though he wanted to seize the helpless Julian.

Then Lewis reasoned and moved. There was one slender, fleeting chance. The door of the office was open. If he could get inside and lock it, the telephone would be his. He could call the police. He could talk to the Consul, and now the Consul would have something to listen to. He would have minutes at least before they broke down the door and hauled him out.

Larreta was coming along the corridor, but Larreta knew only that he was wanted urgently in the sick-room and he swerved to let the desperate man pass.

There was no key in the antique lock of the office; no way of securing the door except by a chair under the handle.

Lewis took that one precaution and dashed to the telephone. The chair was not enough. He needed something to check the inevitable attack. He cursed Julian's passion for antique locks. He cursed the sluggishness of the rural exchange. He gripped the receiver tightly, waiting for an answer. He wrenched open the drawer of the desk with his free hand.

A man fond of pistols might have more than one in the house. But there was nothing in the drawer; only some papers and a few round green pebbles. And Manuel was at the door, shouting wildly and shoving with all his strength against the impeding chair.

No answer came from the exchange. Lewis worked the cradle of the receiver violently. Then he saw that the chair-legs were slipping on the polished floor. He crashed the receiver down, grasped a heavy ebony ruler, and sprang to meet the houseboy.

Caught off balance as the door flew open too suddenly, Manuel offered an easy target for the ruler. He thudded to the floor, and there was no one behind him in the corridor. Lewis ran back to the phone and this time he heard a faint voice on the humming line.

"*Policia !*" he shouted. "*Pronto ! Policia ! Policia.*"

Then Leite was in the room, calling to him to stop and struggling to get the receiver away from him.

When he saw the doctor and two of the men-servants behind her, he gave up. Manuel was on his feet again, and Manuel had murder in his eyes. Before anyone thought of intervening, he lurched across the room and leaped at Lewis, forcing him back across the desk with fingers fastening on his throat.

A sharp command came from Leite. Then, as the Indians seized the houseboy and pulled him back, she turned on him in a fury.

"Keep your hands off him, you snapping dog! I'll have you tied up. Do you hear me? Tied up!"

"We'll see who'll be tied up when Pascual returns."

"Throw him out!" she ordered the Indians.

They forced him through the doorway with obvious reluctance. Doña Leite had to be obeyed, but Manuel was still Manuel.

"Leite, please control yourself," the doctor begged. "This is something for me to handle."

He looked as if he needed a measure of control himself. He was quaking as he faced the defeated Lewis. His thin voice trembled so that his words came with difficulty.

"Señor Page, I am amazed that you should behave in this way after our talk together."

"Be amazed," Lewis retorted. "I don't want to hear any more of your talk. I've heard enough from my brother."

"Señor Page, you will listen to me. Then, if you care to, you may telephone the police or anyone you wish."

"You will listen," Leite insisted, and, with the two Indians holding him, Lewis was left with no choice.

"I warned you clearly enough," Larreta complained. "The damage you have done by encouraging your brother to over-tax his strength may be beyond repair. I, certainly, will take no responsibility for the consequences."

"He wanted me to know the truth," Lewis answered hotly. "Now I know it."

"The truth? You have a super-intelligence, señor, if you can distinguish the truth from the hallucinations of a sick man. I told you that the end of the coma might disclose a changed mental attitude. I do not know what happened to send you shouting for the police, but it is very plain that you are the victim of the deterioration in your brother's mind. A man who comes suddenly from the fantasies of delirium may easily confuse those fantasies with reality."

"Is that all you have to say?"

"It should be enough for a reasonable man."

"If you are a reasonable man, you can have no objection to my calling the police. You can tell them that I am subject to hallucinations, if you wish. Let them decide between fantasy and reality. I have listened to you. Now I will use the telephone."

"No!" Leite interposed. "I forbid it."

Larreta shrugged and walked from the office, asserting that he was needed in the sick-room.

Lewis faced Leite.

"So you will stand aside, señora, while your husband is being poisoned?"

She looked at him for a long time before she answered in a quiet voice.

"Your brother is not being poisoned. The doctor has told you the truth."

"I think you believe it, señora. I am almost convinced that you do. If I am right, you are being deluded. Nothing is wrong with my brother's mind."

He was sure of it then and he maintained it later, even when he recalled the seeming gibberish that had come from Julian. He believed there was some meaning to those scrambled sounds, but no pondering could give him a clue to it. He tried to repeat the syllables, to write them down before he forgot them.

E-zar . . . e-zar-zar-zar . . .

It had been laid down that he should not visit the sick-room again except in the company of the doctor, and now he was under close guard, watched whenever he moved. As he paced the floor of his room, he was aware that one of the Indians was standing outside the door, and he had the thought that, when Benevides returned from the valley, the room might become his cell, with the key on the outside of the door.

He had demanded news of Julian and had been told that a serious relapse had occurred. The sick man was unconscious again, his condition critical. If he died . . .

Someone knocked. Lewis hesitated. Leite called his name and he opened the door.

She handed him a slip of tinted paper.

"I am sorry," she said. "My brother must have taken it." She was embarrassed. "I didn't know," she added.

He read the message from Anne.

FLYING NEW YORK TONIGHT SAILING BY ATACAMA TUESDAY SEE
YOU SOON ALL LOVE TO YOU AND UNCLE JULIAN

To-day was Wednesday. The *Atacama* was on her way, speeding down towards Panama.

He looked up to find Leite's troubled gaze upon him.

"Why did you have to come here?" she cried. "Why did you?"

She was gone before he could think of anything to say. Then he worried over her, wondering why she was in such torment. He was sure that she had no love for Julian. She had shown not even pity for the sick man; rather revulsion. Julian for her was a means to an end, and the end was something designed by Benevides.

Lewis was in torment himself. It was treachery to Julian to give a thought of sympathy to the woman. Instead of probing for a hidden meaning, he should have taken her question literally and answered it accordingly.

"I came here to borrow money, but that's of no account now. I'm staying here to save Julian's life, and I'm staying till I am sure he is out of danger. I'll find some way. You may be certain of that."

He was certain of it himself. As soon as night came he would break out of his prison. He would risk the bullets of any guards that he might encounter, but he had the belief that he could evade them.

The trees grew thickly at the end of the drive, and under cover of darkness he must succeed. By the time the moon rose he would be far down the road to Trajano, away from these barbarous hills.

"I must save him," he repeated to himself. "I will save him."

He felt the power in him, but it was a delusion. Before the night came, Julian was dead.

CHAPTER XIV

WITH BERMUDA already far astern and the *Atacama* heading towards the Bahamas, Anne wished only to rest in her deck-chair and go over the pleasures derived from her first port of call. The "Principles of Orchestration" slipped from her lap and thudded on the deck, and Rimsky-Korsakov was supplanted in her mind by Andrew Marvell. She saw in shades the orange bright like golden lamps in a green night, although she had encountered no oranges in Hamilton outside of a fruit shop. But more pertinent, perhaps, was the poet's image of eternal spring.

"You dropped your book, señorita. Permit me."

Unless you retired to your cabin, you could get no privacy for reflection. Hemmed in by a New World Latin on one side and an American type on the other – both of them youthful, self-confident and aspiring – she was constantly obliged to suffer their unwanted social advances.

No doubt they looked on her as a shy creature. Or they might even put her down as a bit of a snob. Anyway, she had no intention of wasting the days of this voyage on shuffle-board and deck tennis. She had her string quartet to think of, and there was the bruised Rimsky to study. And she still felt the stimulation of those remote Bermudas. A choral setting of Marvell's "Song of the Emigrants" was quite a possibility.

"Will you come up for the dance to-night, Anne?"

It was, perhaps, the assumption of all Americans that they could call you by your Christian name, no matter how short the acquaintance.

"I don't think so, Mr. Wayne." She stressed the note of formality, then, fearing that she was overdoing the chill a little, she added: "I'm not a very good dancer."

"Impossible, señorita!" her neighbour on the right protested.

The name on the passenger list was Mr. S. Byrne, but the stewards always addressed him with some deference as Don Sebastian. And Don Sebastian had described himself as an opera singer, so there was some ground for accord between them, however hedged it might be by the disdain of the creative musician for the mere interpreter. It was also in his favour that he could talk of San Mateo with the familiarity of a native son.

"With your form and your grace of movement, señorita, you are born to dance," Don Sebastian insisted.

Anne laughed. A witty retort in deprecation might be beyond her, but at least she was learning not to be embarrassed by the extravagant compliments that came so freely from Señor Byrne.

"To-night I will teach you our South American steps." Don Sebastian's eyes were full of admiration. "You will see how easy it is if you will rely on me."

She had no intention of relying on him. With everybody at the dance, she would be able to find a secluded spot on the promenade and plan her new work in peace.

And it was not difficult to find that secluded spot when the time came, but the stars, brighter than she had ever seen them, were distracting and she could not at once recapture a theme that had been running in her head during dinner. She drew a staff on the fly-leaf of a book and jotted down a few notes, but when she hummed them over they were surprisingly like the whisper of a tango that reached her from the boat-deck and not at all a rhythm to guide the chime of Marvell's falling oars.

She tried again. The whisper from the boat-deck was now a rumba and the pulse of the engines brought an effect of fantastic syncopation. She waited till the rumba came to an end, then scribbled some more crotchets and quavers on her staff. When she looked up, Mr. Delbert Wayne was in front of her, staring down at her.

There was always something about young Mr. Wayne that made her feel uneasy. This time she was even a little startled.

"Why aren't you dancing?" she asked him in a tone that should have sent him scurrying.

"Are you dancing?" he inquired. "Why should I be? Anyway, I'm glad you're not. Let's walk, shall we?"

"Mr. Wayne, I'm trying to work."

That should have crushed him, but he refused even to wilt.

"Mr. Wayne?" he echoed with a questioning stress. "Do I have to call you Miss Page, then? All your life?"

His voice had a terrifying earnestness, as if he were looking far beyond the duration of this brief voyage. She knew all about the transience of shipboard relations; how they seldom survived a meeting on shore. And for Mr. Wayne there would not even be a meeting on shore, for he was sailing on, past Santa Teresa, to some remote port in Chile.

All her life? "Why," she said, "we've been acquainted only a few days."

It was prim and prudish, with a crackle of buckram in it, but she could think of nothing else. Not that she was without experience. She had developed an almost automatic method of dealing with boys at the school, and she could manage, she was sure, the mercurial temperament of a Don Sebastian. All tenors were stupid – the Italians had pronounced the word for it – and especially operatic tenors. But Del Wayne was no tenor.

"A few days!" He had a habit of picking up the end of a sentence and adding an exclamation mark in a speculative way. "That's long enough to be friends, isn't it? In a few days you'll be leaving us at Santa Teresa. I want to talk to you."

"Mr. Wayne, I'm trying to fix the theme of an important choral work."

"Can't it wait a few minutes? I never get a chance for a word with you. That confounded opera singer is always –"

That confounded opera singer came swiftly, like a guardian angel suddenly summoned to his job; a guardian angel in a gleaming tropical dinner-jacket.

"Señorita!" he exclaimed. "I have been searching the whole ship. There is just time for a tango. Then I have to do a number with Carmen Carisimo. By special request. It is the zapateado, with the variations of the San Mateo tradition. Señor Wayne will excuse you, I am sure."

He shrugged off the lethal stare of Señor Wayne and hurried her up to the boat-deck. Then, before she could resist, she was drawn into the midst of the dancers.

"That's right," Don Sebastian said. "Relax. Just follow me. In a little while you will be as good as I am myself. In Trajano I will take you to the President's Ball."

It was idle shipboard chatter, of course, but it required an answer. "I'm afraid I shall not spend much time in Trajano," she told him. "A few weeks at the Casa Alta and I'll be on my way back to London."

"No," he protested. "It is destined that we shall meet in Trajano."

She laughed. "You have been looking in a crystal, perhaps?"

"I have no need of crystals. This is a matter of second sight."

He seemed so serious that she drew away a little to look at him. Suddenly, for no reason at all, there was a small fear in her, but she could reassure herself without difficulty. Her immediate future was a matter of a simple itinerary, and Don Sebastian was not in it.

Meanwhile she was content to be in his charge. He was a wonderful dancer, an exemplar of correct behaviour, and no one could deny that he was extremely handsome. Dancing with such a partner was an enjoyable experience, and she was reluctant to let him go to Señorita Carisimo for the special exhibition number.

Carmen Carisimo was waiting with a worried frown on her plump pretty face. She was always worried about something, and this time it was her professional reputation. The bright and particular star of the Trajano Ballet could not afford to take risks.

"You prance like a pig," she charged Sebastian. "You will make a fool of me before these people. It is madness that I appear without my Hilarion."

"This is the zapateado, not 'Swan Lake,'" Sebastian retorted. "As for your Hilarion, he is a fat elephant."

"You! You giraffe! You knock-kneed mule! I will not dance. Tell them to cancel."

It was too late. The announcement had been made, the deck cleared, and the applause of the expectant company had begun. Carmen fixed a professional smile on her face and stepped into the arena with her despised partner.

Anne watched entranced, following the rhythm of the stamping and pattering feet, and it was not until the spectators were calling excitedly for an encore that she became aware of Delbert Wayne at her side.

"How can you throw yourself at that gigolo?" he demanded suddenly.

She was staggered by the impudence of it. She was cold for a moment, then hot.

"Can't you see what a cheap exhibitionist he is?" the reckless Mr. Wayne went on.

Now she needed a really effective retort, and the words that came to her were quite stupidly inadequate.

"I think you're very rude," she said.

"I think you need someone to look after you."

"Yourself, I suppose?"

"It's an idea."

"It doesn't appeal to me."

A crash of applause proclaimed the end of the supplementary dance. Then Carmen and Don Sebastian were coming towards them.

"I'm sorry, Anne." Delbert Wayne was suddenly pleading. "I apologise. I want to talk to you. Let's go down and get a drink."

"Thank you, I don't need a drink."

"Please, Anne! That fellow gives me a pain."

"Is anyone detaining you?"

Rage leaped destructively in the rash young man.

"No, by gosh!" he shouted. "No one's detaining me. Nobody could!"

He went off abruptly and Anne gazed after him, a little frightened. Don Sebastian was very pleased with himself. Carmen smiled unaffectedly, and, without her frown, she was a charming and affable person. Now that it was over, she had praise for her partner's performance, but Anne found it impossible to listen to the talk. When Sebastian asked her to dance again, he had to repeat it.

"Just once more," she agreed.

This time it was a failure. She hesitated and faulted, and finally made the excuse that she was too tired, but it was worry more than tiredness that moved her to escape. She saw the angry Delbert ordering whisky by the gallon and pouring it down as if it were water. She might have gone to the bar to stop him, only Don Sebastian insisted on escorting her to her cabin.

He lingered at the door, praising her dancing. Then, as she was asserting that she wasn't all that good, he reached for her and pulled her into his arms. He kissed her. He tried to kiss her a second time, but she pushed him away violently and slammed the door.

She was indignant. She was shaking from the nervous jolt of it. And she was apprehensive of what her exemplar of correct behaviour would do next. She listened intently. She expected importunities, pleas for forgiveness, but all that reached her through the door was the sound of retreating steps.

The night that had been full of stars and pleasurable excitement was a mess: Don Sebastian slinking off along the alleyway, Del Wayne drinking himself into a stupor, and herself . . . She felt very young and incompetent and scared. It had been a mistake to leave the security of Richmond, to venture all alone on this perilous voyage.

She crossed to the port-hole and made sure that it was fastened. She fiddled with the air-conditioning gadget to get a cooler flow, and suddenly she was rigid at the sound of more steps in the alleyway.

It was definitely not a steward. The knock on the door panel was too tentative, too discreet.

"Go away!" she called.

"Certainly," the voice of Del Wayne replied. "I merely brought your book down. You left it on the deck-chair. I thought the notes you were making might be valuable, and you never know, when you leave things around . . ."

She opened the door and received the precious book.

"It's very good of you. I'm most grateful."

"Not at all. I'm happy to be of service. I hope the work will be a big success."

There was a slight touch of irony in his voice; no trace of alcohol. His smile seemed a little sad, but she might be mistaken in this. She was so often deceiving herself.

"Good night, Miss Page," he said. "Sleep well."

She feared she would not sleep at all, but again she was deceiving herself. She awoke refreshed, most agreeably at ease, and no thought of embarrassment came to her until she left her cabin, late as usual.

Few of the passengers were still at breakfast and she did not see Don Sebastian or Delbert Wayne till she went on deck. Sebastian greeted her with his usual effusiveness, his conscience as unruffled as his sleek hair. Mr. Wayne looked up from a book and mumbled a good morning. He was surly, or merely studious. The book was his favourite work, a monster production on copper and copper-mining.

Don Sebastian attempted a conversation, but Anne opened her own favourite book and produced a pencil and note-paper.

"We are all very busy this morning," Don Sebastian lamented. "I suppose that I, too, should study." He raised a vocal score from the deck beside his chair. "You know *Tosca* of course, señorita? When I sing Cavaradossi in Trajano, you shall have the best seats in the house."

Anne looked up. She had always placed him in minor roles, influenced no doubt by the derisory comments of Mr. Wayne. He was young to be a principal tenor. It took years of training and experience, except in rare cases.

Don Sebastian grinned understandingly. "Yes," he said. "It is to be my grand début. In Italy I was fortunate to be the second anvil in *Trovatore,* but in San Mateo . . ."

Mr. Wayne came up from his copper-mine to complete the sentence.

"In San Mateo it is easier."

Don Sebastian was hurt. "Are you suggesting, señor, that our opera is without distinction? Caruso himself, Scotti, Destinn, Fleta —"

75

Mr. Wayne broke in rudely on the list of the great. "I'm suggesting nothing," he snapped. "You are fortunate. That's all. I congratulate you."

"The insinuation does not escape me, señor." Don Sebastian's face wore a hot flush. "Because my father is the Minister of Fine Arts, you think he controls our State Opera. Let me inform you that it is the public, the audience, that controls the Opera."

"So your engagement is by popular vote? I congratulate you again."

"And your engagement, señor? It is due, perhaps, to a plebiscite of the peons who slave in the copper mines?"

They were bristling like a couple of maddened terriers, glaring redly at one another across the reclining cause of it. Anne wanted to shout at them to stop, but the fear of what might happen next had a paralysing effect on her. She imagined a swift crescendo of personal abuse, a challenge, a duel. The passionate Latin would insist on pistols. Or knives. Turiddu and Alfio, but no music by Mascagni. She looked anxiously along the promenade and saw intervention on the way.

Señorita Carisimo came with a frown of worry deeper than usual.

"Sebastian!" She flourished the ship's radio news-sheet in front of him. "Have you seen this report about the Bartolistas?"

"What?" It took even the mercurial Don Sebastian a moment to disengage his mind from an intense hatred of his rival. "What is it?" he demanded in Spanish.

"The Bartolistas," Carmen repeated tragically. "Here, in the ship's news!"

"I have seen it." Don Sebastian brushed the paper away impatiently. "Why do you get yourself in a panic over such an absurdity?"

"Is it an absurdity that a gun-runner has been arrested?" Carmen's voice rose to a near scream. "Izarbarra is in Trajano."

"False, false!" Don Sebastian laughed. "Izarbarra would not dare to show himself in San Mateo. You have nothing to worry about. How can you imagine for a moment that an insurrection could succeed? Our government is the most popular in all our history. We have increased the civil service by one hundred per cent. We have appointed more new letter-carriers than any previous administration. Who is to revolt?"

"Bartol will come back. He has sworn it."

"Izarbarra has sworn it, and what is the worth of his oath?"

"He has been seen in Trajano. On the Plaza Bolivar itself. In disguise."

"Disguise! How then could he have been recognised? It is all the imagination of that imbecile Gonzales. Every week he fills his paper with a lot of alarmist nonsense."

"I do not want to go to Trajano. I have been through one revolution. That is enough."

"I tell you there will be no revolution. It is the height of folly to be a coward when there is no need for cowardice."

Carmen stamped angrily. "I am no coward. I have my career to think of. I can get a contract for Buenos Aires."

Don Sebastian stamped figuratively in return. "*Madre de Dios!* How can you think that Bartol will ever come back. He is a fat playboy who would run at the sound of a gun."

"And you? You are a blind moron, an ignorant mule. I am sending a radio message at once. I will leave the ship at Cristobal and fly to Buenos Aires."

"You are mad. You have signed for the season in Trajano. You will be sued for breach of contract."

"That will be better than a stray bullet. I have no wish to be blown up by a home-made bomb."

She wheeled and started urgently along the deck. Sebastian sprang from his chair, overtook her, and held her in argument.

Delbert Wayne turned to Anne.

"Did you understand what they said?" he asked anxiously.

"Some of it." She affected indifference. "It's no concern of mine what they say to one another. Anyway, I can't follow everything when they talk so fast."

"I can. It's part of my job to know Spanish." Quickly he translated the more alarming phrases, and he seemed more worried than Carmen herself. "I can't bear to think of your going to that place if there's going to be trouble."

"You don't have to think about it. I'm not afraid. My father would have cabled me if there were any real danger. My Uncle Julian would have seen to that."

"Wait!"

He was gone for ten minutes. He came back with a copy of the ship's news and he seemed reassured.

"Perhaps it is just a lot of scare stuff," he said. "I had a word with that Colombian journalist. All the same, I wish you were not going to San Mateo."

"Why do you have to worry about me?"

Her look was meant to wither him, and he was withered. He returned to his copper-mine with an inarticulate ejaculation, half sad, half angry.

New Providence was near. She closed her book and joined the throng of passengers at the rail. She was determined now to avoid both troublesome swains, so when the ship came into Nassau she went sight-seeing with a French doctor and his wife.

Back on board, with Andros gliding away aft, Don Sebastian found her.

"I hope you had an interesting time," he said. "I wished to take you ashore, but I had to cling to Carmen. It is important that she does not desert us for Buenos Aires. She is needed in Trajano. Did you see the sponge market?"

"Yes, thank you."

"But Havana will be the great day. We will have a wonderful time. You will be my guest?"

"No."

"Of course you will, my dear Anne."

"No."

She was less emphatic when Delbert Wayne came to her with a similar invitation. He seemed so contrite for his behaviour in the morning that she was a little sorry for him, and her gentleness must have suggested irresolution.

"I know the place quite well," he urged in his best Harvard manner. "It would be a great pleasure to show you round."

"I'm sorry. I've already arranged."

"With Señor Byrne, I suppose?"

His flash of jealousy brought back alarm in her, but she was firm.

"Mr. Wayne, if I go ashore at all, it will be with Dr. Planchard and his wife."

It had a final sound, but unfortunately the Planchards made no approach to her. Possibly they had had enough of her at Nassau. Or, as newly-weds, they found adequate company in one another. Anne was unwanted by all except Mr. Wayne and Don Sebastian.

And Mr. Wayne had the edge in an obstinate refusal to admit defeat. Even when they were in sight of Morro Castle he was still urging his proficiency as a guide, and the prospect of wandering alone in the unknown streets of Havana was too frightening. She surrendered.

The sequel surprised her. Del was really quite charming when you got to know him. And amusing. He kept her happy and laughing, though she sometimes had a pang of conscience over the money he was spending. It might be that he drew a good salary from that copper mine down in Chile, but surely not enough to support such extravagance! When he wished to buy a gift for her, she protested. She was, indeed, a little indignant. This was going altogether too far for a stranger.

Nevertheless, as they stood by the rail together and watched the coastline of Cuba fading into a shadow astern, her response to his friendliness was less reluctant than it had been, and she dressed more carefully than usual for dinner that night. She had promised to dance with him, and, after the glorious day he had given her, she felt that she must reward him by looking her best.

The matter was of no consequence, of course. She would soon be forgotten. When she stepped ashore at Santa Teresa . . .

Santa Teresa?

Goodness! The cable she had planned to send from Havana had quite slipped her mind.

She looked at her watch. She had to meet Del in the cocktail bar before dinner, but there was still time enough. She went up to the wireless cabin and asked the officer if he could take a message for San Mateo.

CHAPTER XV

MANUEL BROUGHT the radio-telegram to Lewis. "It has been opened in error," he said. "Don Pascual thought it was another word of condolence, but it is good news. I took the liberty to read it. You will pardon me, I hope."

The houseboy grinned impudently. "You will see that your little daughter is enjoying the voyage," he went on. "She had a very happy day in Havana. I am not surprised. Havana is a nice place for young people."

Lewis took the typewritten sheet and read Anne's brief message. There was nothing more in it than Manuel had recited. "All my love to you and Uncle Julian," it ended. "Dying to see you both."

"The *Atacama* will be at Santa Teresa in three days' time," Manuel said. "It is a pity that the young lady will meet with such sad news on her arrival."

"Tell señor Benevides that I wish to leave for Trajano this evening. No, wait. I'll tell him myself."

Lewis had a feeling of relief. However deeply he must mourn the loss of Julian, at least this ordeal of subjection to Benevides would soon be over, for Leite had assured him that he would be free to meet Anne.

"My brother wishes you to stay only until the lawyer has been to see us," she had told him. "He wants you to know that everything is in order."

There had been no trace of a widow's grief in her, but he had been left without doubt of her sympathy for him.

"You will believe, please, that I feel for you in your distress," she had added. "I have made my brother promise that you will not be hampered any more."

They had buried Julian with correct ceremony in the little cemetery outside the village of Rosario. An Anglican vicar had been brought from Trajano to read the service, and Lewis had attended the heavily-veiled Leite at the graveside. Benevides had gone off to the jungle early in the morning and had not returned.

For once there had been no guard in evidence at the entry to the drive, but Manuel and one of the workmen had kept close watch on Lewis, ready to intervene, it seemed, if he tried to give a message to the vicar.

The next day the lawyer had come, a bleak, sallow man, in a hurry to dispatch his business and get away, Lewis had been summoned to the office to be told the contents of the will.

Nothing could have been more simply framed. There were legacies of one hundred pounds each to Lewis and Anne, and all the rest was left to Leite.

"Here is the original testament," the lawyer said; "and here is the English translation. I wish Señor Page to understand that his brother transferred his legal business to me at the time of his marriage. The will conforms to the settlement drawn up by myself. You will observe, Señor Page, that it is dated three days after the ceremony."

He paused while Lewis inspected the will.

"You had better examine this, also," Benevides remarked, pushing a paper towards him.

It was a certificate of civil marriage, attested by a local magistrate.

Lewis looked at the date, then at the will again. He could not doubt that the signature was Julian's.

"I understand there was a previous will," the lawyer said, "but I know nothing of its terms. As it is revoked by the present instrument, there is no point in making a search. If Señor Page has any questions, I will try to answer them."

Lewis had no questions. Substance in black and white could not be challenged by a shadow of suspicion.

"Then there is nothing more to detain me." The lawyer gathered his papers and turned to Benevides. "I will put through the formalities as quickly as possible."

Lewis had taken doubts with him from the meeting. He had tried to resolve them, tried to resign himself to the hopelessness of his position, but they were still with him as he folded Anne's radio message and went in search of Benevides. Whatever game these people were playing, it seemed clear that they had gained complete dominance over Julian. What he could not determine was whether they had practised fraud and gone on to something worse.

"Don Pascual is in the solana," Manuel said.

Benevides and Leite were both in the sun-parlour and the atmosphere within the room was as heavy with storm as the clouds that hung a dark curtain beyond the panorama of the mountain.

Lewis hesitated at the door, aware that he was interrupting another of their scenes. The troubled Leite urged him to come in as though she welcomed his intervention.

Benevides wheeled angrily. "What do you want now, señor?" he demanded.

Lewis decided to be as polite as he could. He apologised for intruding. As there was no reason why he should prolong his stay, perhaps señor Benevides would be good enough to place a car at his disposal or permit him to telephone to the man who had brought him from Trajano.

"When do you wish to leave?"

"This evening, or to-morrow morning at the latest."

"To-morrow morning at the latest!" The echo had an ominous inflection. "This is to be regretted, señor. Are you not pleased with our hospitality? You have the freedom of the house. You may come and go on the estate as you wish."

"You are aware, señor, that I have to meet my daughter at Santa Teresa."

"I am not aware that it is necessary. I have assured you that your daughter will be cared for."

"I prefer to care for her myself." Lewis glanced at Leite and saw her quick anger focusing on Benevides. "As everything is now settled," he added, "I wish to leave at once."

"It is not convenient."

"But —"

"I say it is not convenient."

Leite intervened, and her Spanish had a whip-lash violence. "What is this? You promised me there would be no more of this madness. I have given my word to him."

"Then you can take it back." Benevides was equally violent. "The madness is in you. Do you want this man to ruin everything, now that we have gone so far? His purpose is not to meet his daughter. It is to run to the police with his story of poison. You know his insane suspicion. He has done nothing but make trouble all the time he has been here."

"It is you who gave him cause to —"

"Be quiet! You are well aware that we can take no chances. Once loose, he will raise heaven and earth and the devil himself. He will go to his Consul, and next thing the police will be here to exhume the body."

"One moment," Lewis put in. "I have no intention of going to the police or the Consul. I wish only to meet my daughter and leave San Mateo as soon as I can make arrangements."

Benevides swung round on the first word and stared at him.

"So you understand our language, Señor Page? Perhaps you also speak it? You have been remarkably quiet about it all this time. It has been convenient for you to spy on us, no doubt!"

"You are mistaken. I was unaware . . ."

"Please!" Leite cut in on him sharply and turned on Benevides again. "Why do you have to stir up fresh suspicion? Señor Page has given you his word. He is satisfied. The estate is now in my charge and you have authority to go on with your work. Isn't that enough for you?"

"It is not enough. I must protect your interests and mine till the work is complete. I am not concerned about your petty inheritance as the widow of Julian Page any more than you are. The Izarbarra and Mayorga estates are themselves a mere bagatelle."

Izarbarra!

Julian's meaningless stammer clicked into the name. Lewis felt a shock of nervous apprehension. Somewhere he had heard or seen the name.

Izarbarra . . .

Only by an effort could he concentrate on what Benevides was saying. He caught dimly a pertinent phrase and had to repeat it to himself before he could grasp its significance.

"Señor Page will stay here until I myself can see that he is put on board a ship for England."

Lewis was dimly aware that a storm had broken over the mountains. He blinked as lightning lit up the dusk of the sun-parlour. He saw the troubled, angry face of Leite and his one thought then was that he must protect her from the rage she had provoked in Benevides. Distant thunder echoed along the deep valleys, but the sharp, rising voice of Benevides had a more menacing sound.

"Do you hear, Señor Page? You will stay in this house for the present."

"Then what is to be done about my daughter?" Lewis demanded.

"I have already told you. I will care for her."

"Will you bring her here?"

"I will consider it." Then, in sudden fury: "Damn your daughter! Have I nothing else to think of? This is enough."

"No!" Again Leite objected. "It is not enough. You will order the car for Don Lewis, or I will leave you this night."

"And where will you go?"

"To Maria Josefa."

"How? Will you walk? You may try the ravine, but the cliff is perpendicular and there is no foothold. The alternative is the jungle, but no one has ever got through the jungle alive. The way by the road is closed. To everybody."

"You will not dare to hold me here."

"What is daring about it? I think you are a little feverish, Leite. It would be well if Dr. Larreta took a look at you."

"So!" She jerked her head back nervously as if she had received a blow. She was rigid, staring at Benevides, unable to believe what the suggestion conveyed to her. Then incredulity became conviction and she reacted in a passion that ignored the presence of Lewis.

"So it is true!" she cried. "Maria Josefa was right. All the time she has seen the truth, and I would not listen to her. You brought Larreta here to use him as . . ."

"Silence!" he broke in on her. "Keep your devil's tongue quiet!"

"You are not going to frighten me! You've deceived and used me as you've used all the others, Enrique among them. What will you do when the time comes and Enrique returns? Will you have your medico ready with his needle? Will you murder Enrique, too?"

Benevides moved swiftly and his hands were on her throat. No lightning came from the storm clouds over the mountains, but something seemed to flash before the eyes of Lewis and he was quite berserk, with only the thought of Leite in his mind.

He leaped forward, swinging wildly, and Don Pascual went down, overturning a table with a crash. Lewis fell on top of him, grappling with his left hand, striking with his right fist.

Leite screamed a warning and Lewis saw the glint of a knife. He grasped at the wrist of the threatening hand, but he knew at once that he had not the strength to control Benevides. Leite knew it too, and hammered at the hand with a glass ash-tray. The knife fell from numbed fingers. Lewis grappled again, but the next instant he was hauled from his enemy by Manuel.

Benevides rose quickly, kicked the heavy ash-tray aside, and picked up his knife. Now he was slow and deliberate in movement. He looked down at his bruised fingers, then gazed at Leite and stepped towards her, holding out the hand for her inspection.

He said: "Do you see what you have done?"

She was silent, afraid, but she would not retreat.

"It is well for you that there are no bones broken," he told her quietly. "The hand is still strong. You see?"

She rocked back from the force of the blow as he slapped her face, but still she would give no ground.

"You see?" He struck her a second blow, and this time she was rock still.

"You make it clear," she said. "You make everything clear."

"That will do for you. There will be no more treachery. You are under orders, like the rest. My orders. You are not here to question. You are here to serve."

He moved towards the door without a glance at Lewis.

"All right, Manuel," he said. "You can let that fellow go. I will deal with him later. Let him go. I want you in the office."

Manuel followed him.

Sound to Lewis seemed distant, muted by the murmur of a sea. Then he became aware that it was raining; that the murmur was the drumming of the heavy downpour on the flat roof.

Leite moved slowly towards the great window, and he saw her figure in silhouette against the streaming world outside. The panorama of mountains and cloud had disappeared.

For a long time she stood there, staring at the rain. Then, without turning, she spoke, and it seemed to him that she must have known what was in his mind.

"You will not attempt anything," she said. "If you do, they will shoot you down."

He took a step towards her. It was difficult to make his voice reach her through the sound of the rain.

"I must get to Santa Teresa," he answered her.

"I am trying to tell you that they will kill you." Again she did not turn. "You have heard too much."

All the heat had left him. The chill he felt was fear.

"What is the meaning of it?" he asked.

He was groping. He could not think clearly because fear was an impediment to thought. He was certain now that Julian had been murdered, and he knew that she, too, believed it.

She did not answer his question. "Leave me!" she cried suddenly, and there was an imperative edge to the demand.

He went from the sun-parlour to his own room, trying to control himself. He stood for a long time by his window, seeing nothing, not even realising that the rain had stopped until he saw Benevides and Manuel in the forecourt.

They passed quickly and took the path along the valley between the terraces where the coffee berries were withering under the dripping guamo trees.

Lewis heard again the resolution of Julian's stammered syllables in the sharp acid voice of Benevides.

Izarbarra!

The sky was a pale wash of blue after the storm and the air had a golden glow. The stone shapes of the gods and warriors, still glistening with the water on them, steamed under the hot sun.

Izarbarra . . .

He had it. He reached for the wallet in his breast pocket and unfolded the page he had torn from the Trajano newspaper to keep for Anne.

On the reverse of the article about Avila, the composer, was the picture of ex-President Bartol and his former cabinet.

Lewis read the cut-line, and the name was there among the others: Minister of Public Security, Alonzo Pascual Izarbarra.

He skimmed the vituperative article till he found the name again.

The man most to be feared among the bandit gang is Izarbarra, the cut-throat instigator of the crimes that brought obloquy to the name of Bartol and led to his overthrow. The hand of this ruthless monster is behind the new conspiracy and our Government must not be lulled to sleep by a false sense of security. The price on his head will not stop Izarbarra. We are satisfied with our evidence that he has returned to San Mateo, and, unless the utmost vigilance is maintained, Bartol will follow when the time is ripe. We utter this solemn warning to President Recalde.

Lewis examined the half-tone reproduction of the group and focused on the face of Izarbarra. The epithets of the writer were in his mind, but he needed no borrowed terms to establish the countenance of cruelty. The eyes were menacing under the heavy level brows, the narrow nose had a predatory look, the bushy moustache bristled above the thin line of the mouth.

Only the moustache was strange to Lewis. The rest was the face of Benevides.

Hints, the remembered details of a letter, of phrases heard, came together to construct a coherent story.

Izarbarra was the man who had forced Julian to give him shelter when the fleeing Bartolistas were being hunted by the triumphant Recalde party.

"Once Julian saved my life," Benevides had said.

And Julian had found it all very amusing, a comic opera revolution. He had no doubt looked upon the refugee with the threatening pistol as a comedian. "A fantastic fellow," he had written. "I gave him a meal and showed him a hole where he could hide ... I hope he got away safely. I never saw him again."

Years ago, but Izarbarra had come back. Izarbarra had seen the value of the lonely coffee finca run by the eccentric Englishman. A safe spot, a hidden centre for the organisation of another coup. And Izarbarra had been prepared to use any means to gain possession: first the charms of Leite and then the poisons of Dr. Larreta.

Lewis shivered. He was the one man who could destroy the plot, but he was securely held, and when Anne landed at Santa Teresa she would become a hostage for his silence.

He left the house and walked in the sun, seeking warmth to drive the coldness out of him. His fear would not respond. It was like the ice on the farthest mountain peaks.

An Indian woman came from the kitchen quarters and plodded along the path to the jungle. The guamo trees were still steaming after the rain.

Lewis looked up into the malignant face of a stone image that stared out across the valley. It might serve, he thought, as the genius of this land, of this small fragment broken from the Empire of the Andes. Liberator would follow liberator, the Bartols and the Recaldes would come and go, but it was all unimportant to this god that Julian had unearthed. It was unimportant to all but those who were caught in the trap.

He did not see Leite until she spoke to him.

"There is only one way for you," she said. "You must try to get through the jungle. I have made what arrangements I can. There is a man who has been driven from the house by my brother. He lives among the trees and I have sent to him the woman that feeds him. If he will help you, you may reach Santa Teresa in time. If you stay here, you will have no chance of anything."

She was talking rapidly as if she feared that Benevides might be returning along the valley path at any moment.

"The way is left open because it is thought that no one can get through the jungle alive. I do not believe it. Nothing is impossible if you have the will and the knowledge. This man has the knowledge, if only he will guide you. Please listen carefully to everything I say."

Lewis listened carefully. The Indian woman came back along the valley path and Leite beckoned to her.

"Well, Yerma?"

"I do not know." The woman's voice had deep anxiety in it. "He will not say yes; he will not say no. He has waited all this time to reach the road to Rosario."

"Doesn't he know that he will never reach the road?"

"That I told him. He is very patient."

"There is no time for patience." Leite turned to Lewis. "We will have to persuade him. Perhaps for your brother's sake he will consent. Immediately after dinner will be the time to set out. If luck is with you, no one will miss you till morning. Do you understand everything I have told you?"

He understood.

After dinner he changed his shoes for stout walking boots. Manuel watched him leave the house, but Lewis had made a habit of an evening walk, so Manuel merely grinned and warned him mockingly to be wary of the night air. Manuel was so certain that there was no way of escape, and perhaps he was right.

Lewis sauntered along the gravel, pausing once to light his pipe. When he reached the end of the forecourt he looked back, but no shadow showed against the lighted front of the house.

He took the path along the valley. He counted the guamo trees on his right. Under the tenth tree he found a bundle done up in a thick poncho, and, shouldering it, he quickened his pace.

There was no hitch; no one to impede him. When he came to the end of the path at the edge of the ravine, he struck a match, held it up for a moment, and threw it away. Another match; then a third.

"Don Lewis!"

He heard again the once familiar voice of Julian's houseboy, and he wheeled, startled, as a figure emerged from the dark bush close to him.

"Pepe!" Surprise gave exclamatory force to the name. "It is you?"

"Yes, señor. I knew you had come back to the house, but I could not go to you. I have been hunted like an animal. But for the help of the girl Yerma, I would not be alive."

"Pepe! What happened to you?"

"It was the day of the fight, señor. The man Izarbarra came to make trouble. Don Julian tried to phone for the police. Izarbarra seized him and they fought. I did my best to help, but that Manuel was there and almost before I could cry out, Don Julian was stabbed. Then the house was full of Izarbarra's men. I thought that Don Julian was dead, and I believed that I, too, would be killed. I ran, and they fired at me. One bullet hit me, but I ran on. They were swarming over the grounds like an army: fifty, sixty men from the camp they have made in the hills. There was only one way I could run from them. Once I reached the jungle, I was safe."

Pepe pointed vaguely. "I lived in the hole where we hid the snake Izarbarra after the victory of the Recaldistas. The first day I was sick from the bullet. The wound was here, through the flesh of the leg. It was stiff and painful, but clean. In the night I limped to the house to get food and other things from Yerma. Each night she has brought me food and drink."

He laughed. "It is good to have a woman. Sometimes they are useful."

"How long have you been living like this?" Lewis asked him.

"All of four weeks, señor. The fight was at the beginning of the month. Two days after it, men came to the hole and began to dig. I was away at the spring for water, or they would have caught me. They

found my poncho and bits of food I had left. Then they hunted and
hunted, but when they failed in their hunt they went back to their
digging and I moved to another hole. Why do they dig every day, Don
Lewis? There are no more gods in that place."

"I don't know. The path is guarded."

"That I have seen. There are many things I cannot understand.
Yerma tells me what goes on, but she is not very clever in the head.
First Izarbarra tries to kill Don Julian; then he moves heaven and earth
to save him. For days and days the doctor lives in the house."

Pepe shook his head. "Another strange thing is this Doña Leite.
Don Julian never told me that he would take a wife. All the years I
worked for him, he seemed not to worry about women. When was the
marriage?"

"Three weeks ago. They brought a magistrate to the house."

"A magistrate! That is why Yerma knew nothing about it. If it had
been a priest . . . But she says it is only in the last few days that she has
seen this Doña Leite. She is kept in the kitchen, of course. She does
not see everything."

"Doña Leite has been away. Perhaps she came only for the marriage
and had to leave at once."

Perhaps he was trying to answer his own doubts.

"Yes," Pepe agreed. "Don Julian must have known that he would
die, so he sent for her. Yerma says she is a good woman."

"I believe she is, Pepe. I believe she is."

"Why do you say it like that, Don Lewis?"

"Because I, too, find things that are difficult to understand."

"Sometimes marriages are sudden. That is as God wills. But it is
most strange that I have never seen Doña Leite."

"You will see her very soon. She is coming with your Yerma to
bring us more food."

"Coming here!" Pepe was alarmed. "Señor, it could be a trap. If she
has tricked Yerma, she could lead the others here. They will kill me for
what I have seen. They have had men all along the road so that I
should not reach the police."

The stars gave enough light to show Lewis that the man was

frightened, and he agreed to wait alone on the path while Pepe went some distance towards the house to make sure that the women came alone.

When they did come, Leite, cloaked in a poncho, was scarcely distinguishable from the Indian. Pepe reappeared at once, but he seemed only partly satisfied. For a long moment he peered at Leite. Then he spoke.

"Señora, I have decided. I will try the jungle with Don Lewis. Perhaps we shall get through. If it is impossible, we will return. Don Lewis will be safe with me, even if we have to live in the jungle for many days."

"I shall not turn back," Lewis asserted. "I must get through."

"We have brought enough food for three days," Leite told him. "There are two pairs of leggings in your poncho."

"They will be necessary, señora." Pepe spoke nervously and looked back along the path. "We will go now to my hiding-place and at dawn we will start. It is best that you return to the house at once."

"Yerma will return. I am going with you."

The quiet assertion so startled Lewis that he could only stare at her, but Pepe exploded violently.

"*Madre de Dios*, it is impossible! The jungle will take all the strength of men. You do not know what you are saying."

"I have strength," she answered icily. "I can go wherever you go."

"You have great courage, señora, but . . ."

"I am going with you." She turned to Lewis. "If I have courage, it is because I am afraid to stay. I have come to an end with my brother, and I wish to live.'

"But surely there is no question of your safety?" Anxiety for her was suddenly very deep in Lewis. Pepe was frowning and shaking his head.

"There is no safety anywhere for me," Leite answered. "What will you do if you reach Trajano? You will go to the police, and that will bring the finish. Pascual will know. He will kill me."

"The police cannot bring Julian back to life. I shall not go to them. I give you my word."

"And this man who knows so much?"

"Pepe will obey me."

"All the demons!" Pepe swore. "Will I ever understand what goes on?"

"You must return," Lewis urged her.

"No. I have come too far. Do *you* not understand? Can't you see how I have been deceived? A promise was made to me and it has not been kept. Do you wish to know any more? I was told that your brother was dying. Not that he would be murdered."

She turned to the Indian woman commandingly.

"Go back! If you say one word, you will be punished."

"And do no business with the insurgent scum," Pepe added. "If you are untrue to me, I will cut your throat."

Yerma made a whimpering noise that might have been a protestation of love, but Pepe, without an embrace, waved her on her way.

"Let us start," Leite said sharply.

Pepe looked at her in the starlight, taking her full measure, observing the tough slacks and leather leggings below the folds of her poncho.

"Pardon, señora," he said in his thin voice, "I take no orders from you. Not that I am a politician. It is only that I hate the Bartolistas. You will please remember that I am the servant of Don Lewis."

"Enough!" Lewis snapped. "You will treat Doña Leite with respect."

"Yes, señor. I am always respectful, as you know. And with all respect I suggest that I am in command until we are through this jungle."

Leite laughed. There may have been a little hysteria in it, but to Lewis the laughter was like a breaking of ice. She was human. He saw her again as he had seen her in that plane from Cristobal.

"Come!" Pepe commanded. "Till the morning we will rest in my cave."

CHAPTER XVI

THE WAY WAS EASY on this first stage. They followed the yellow beam of a fading torch through yielding foliage that closed in behind them. The direction was eastward, away from the Casa Alta, but, before the end, Pepe made an abrupt turn to the right and brought them to a cavern-like hole in a creeper-covered wall of rock.

"You must get some sleep," Pepe ordered. "No one will come here."

He had the gift of dropping off at will. Lewis followed Leite's example and spread his poncho so that he could lie on part of it and cover himself with the rest, but neither of the two found it possible to sleep. They waited through the night until Pepe ceased to snore, and that was only when he sprang up, roused suddenly as if by an alarm-clock.

"In a half-hour it will be light," he announced. "Then we must move."

He made coffee over a miniature spirit-stove and they ate and drank. Next he apportioned the burdens of each of them, rolling the stores in the ponchos and strapping them so that they could be slung from the shoulder.

Leite had thought of the straps. She had thought, too, of other things: a revolver and cartridges, sharp-edged machetes, a compass, pocket torches, a portable water-bag.

Pepe thrust the revolver into his belt, nodded his grizzled head appreciatively, and twisted his lined, dark-tanned face into a grin.

"We start," he said.

The faint glimmer of light increased slowly to a green dusk in the first hour, and the way was still comparatively easy. Leite followed the path-finder and Lewis came after her. They had to crush through the meeting fronds of giant ferns and follow a sinuous line between the slender trunks of close-growing trees that rose high in their urge to find light.

Covering the ground was a thick dark litter of fallen leaves through which they must wade as through the water of a shallow ford, but beneath the litter and the pressed layer of mould on which it rested, the earth was firm.

For some time they made good progress. Then their way was hampered by thick screens of twining lianas that hung like giant curtains from the topless trees.

Pepe swung his machete, cutting out a narrow path.

Lewis relieved him after ten minutes, and at the end of a similarly brief spell Leite insisted on taking a turn. Lewis objected. It was man's work, he argued, but he found no support.

"She would not go back," Pepe growled. "She must do her share."

Lewis knew from the aching of his arm that she could not go on for long. He feared that Pepe meant to punish her because he had not wanted her with them, but Pepe was a wise general and watched her carefully.

"Good," he praised her. "It is true you have strength, but you have done enough. There are hard things ahead of us and you must keep your strength."

A clearer stretch, a dell of ferns on a gigantic scale, gave them a respite, but presently they came upon more lianas, thicker than they had yet encountered and hung like a tapestry with a crazy pattern of light and shade.

Pepe shook his head, but attacked the tangle. By noon they were exhausted and he called for a rest. While they ate a little bread and cheese and drank from the water bag, he stared at the compass thoughtfully.

"Our course has been nearly straight," he commented. "If we can keep to the line, we should come out near the river – if we come out at all."

"How many miles of it are there?" Lewis asked.

"Not many. It is not the miles that matter. Let us go on."

They had seen no living thing except furtive monkeys and the birds that chattered and screeched and sometimes flashed down from the tree-tops in swift loops of colour; but soon after they started again Pepe killed a small viper.

It was a bad snake, he said, but he was not much concerned. To tread on one was dangerous, but they had the protection of stout leather. "We must be wary. The snakes are wary, too." He shrugged. "There are not many in this part of the country. I have hunted them. I know. It is not snakes I fear."

"What do you fear?"

Pepe shook his head, and the furrows of his thin, ageing face were deeper. "All say it is impossible to get through. I have heard you may go so far. Then there is a place that none can pass. Myself, I do not know."

Leite had not spoken a word since early in the day. She continued in silence, as if breath were too valuable to waste in speech, and now Lewis and Pepe became dumb, affected, perhaps, by the stillness of the green world. In the hot hours of midday the birds had ceased to chatter and screech, and for some time the silence was broken only by the slash or chop of a machete and the slush-slush of booted feet through the litter of leaves.

Occasionally a faint rustle told of an animal in the undergrowth, but they saw nothing. Occasionally a grunt came from Pepe, a commentary that the others might interpret as they wished.

They reached a place where there was no longer the resistance of firm earth beneath them. The mould, packed down by the weight of its own accumulation, yielded like foam rubber. Then it broke under their soles and they plunged ankle-deep in mud.

No ray of the sun could penetrate the lofty ceiling of massed foliage, but the jungle steamed in the heat and its many odours mingled in a heavy emanation that made breathing painful: odours of rot and decay, of growing and flowering things, damp ferns and springing saplings and opulent blossoms. And now the jungle possessed a voice in the humming and droning and reedy whirring of insects.

The three trudged on through the atmosphere of a poisonous vapour-bath, sweat running into their eyes and down their faces. Sweat-sodden clothes clung to their limbs, and every few yards they had to change their burdens from one shoulder to the other.

Leite stumbled, and Lewis reached out to save her from a fall, but only when he felt for her hand and pressed it in encouragement did she turn to look at him. Then there was so much gratitude in her eyes that his quick response of sympathy had an intensity that was new to him.

Pepe called a halt and they sat for a few minutes on the rotting trunk of a fallen tree. They sat with eyes closed to rest them from the strain of peering into the green twilight.

When they went on the quagmire was deeper. The glutinous mass closed on them and clung to them and every step entailed a struggle against the suction. Soon they were sinking to the knees, and the effort to withdraw each encumbered foot became so exhausting that they had to pause every few yards.

Pepe grunted and pointed to the right, and the other two followed him in that direction, knowing that he was seeking higher or firmer ground. Presently he shook his head and tried to the left, but everywhere the bed of the slough seemed to be on one level.

There were no more screening lianas to be slashed and parted, but among the trees the dark shaggy fern-trunks stood like an army of giants in their way.

The mud became less dense, less tenacious. They pushed on hopefully, but another torture lay ahead, and soon they were wading through a thigh-deep swamp, their feet catching in tangled roots while swarms of insects stung their hands and faces.

An hour of it, or hours, perhaps! It did not matter any longer whether you measured time in minutes or ages. Lewis closed his eyes to shut out the green glare. When he again looked ahead through narrow-slitted lids, it seemed that some of the furry-gleaming fern-trunks stood higher than their fellows.

It was no illusion. His feet were trudging up a sunken incline, and presently the water was only ankle deep; and Pepe, who had gained a lead of several yards, was already clear of the swamp.

After that, with a firm base to the spongy carpet of leaf-mould, the going was easy. And the birds had started their chattering and screeching again, as though to cheer the plodders on their way.

Pepe looked anxiously at the other two and once more called a halt. They rested. They drank from the waterbag. They struggled on for another hour, and then their way was blocked by a barrier of creeper.

It might have been because it was something new in their experience that they stared at it with sinking hearts. Always they had seen light through the screens of twining lianas. Always the screens had hung in vertical lines, but this was different.

"*Madre de Dios!*"

The words from Pepe were a despairing sigh.

This was very different.

The mass seemed to curve outwards from a lofty height as water curves over the brink of a fall. It was a dark static cataract of green and it reached out to the left and the right as far as the eye could penetrate.

The three moved forward through the deepening dusk of the day's end and saw what they had feared to put into a thought. The mass of creeper hid a perpendicular wall of rock, straight sheared as if by some volcanic freak in the days when the mountains were formed.

Pepe grasped twisted strands of the creeper and climbed hand over hand to test them with his weight. They gave way and he fell, pulling down enough of the greenery to cover him.

"This is our place for the night," he said, as he thrust the stuff aside. "We will make a fire, but not till it is dark. Then no smoke will be seen."

"We may have been followed," Lewis warned him sadly.

"They are not lunatics." Pepe managed a grin. "We are the only mad ones."

Lewis moved away and began to gather dry branches. The night came swiftly and they started their fire. They ate and drank. They wrapped themselves in their ponchos while their clothes dried. They rubbed and scraped the mud from their garments and dressed again.

"The fire must be kept going," Pepe ordered. "Then the wild

animals will not trouble us. You and I will take watch and watch, Don Lewis. The señora is to sleep."

She spoke for the first time in an hour. "I will share."

"The señora will sleep," Pepe insisted. "To-morrow we climb the wall. Or we go back. The first watch is mine. I am an old man. I do not need much sleep; only rest for my bones and a moment to think. I will wake you up at eleven, Don Lewis. At two, I will relieve you."

When Lewis began his turn, Leite was sleeping. The fire had been built up and he saw that it would need no attention for some time. He stood for a while. The dreadful weariness had gone from him, but his body was one ache. He rubbed his stiff limbs and walked a little to get his blood circulating.

He paused beneath the wall and gazed up at it in the light from the fire. His mind was a jumbled fantasy of the day's pains and toils, but one clear thought rose out of the nightmare blur. To-night the *Atacama* would be at Cristobal. To-morrow would bring the passage of the Canal.

To-morrow he must reach Trajano . . .

He returned to the fire and sat down, bending with difficulty. He looked into the jungle and saw glowing eyes staring out of the darkness, but they vanished when he shifted. There was no sound in all the stillness except the occasional screech of a night bird and the deep breathing of the sleeping Pepe.

Leite seemed not to breathe at all. He watched for a movement in her throat as if he had to assure himself that she was living. In the deep sleep of exhaustion the marks of strain had gone from her face. He had never seen her so tranquil, so much at peace, and the glow that her cheeks caught from the fire made her seem almost childlike.

It was no wonder, he thought, that Julian had fallen in love with her beauty. This, at least, was clearly feasible, but it gave no clue to her side of the enigma; her neglect of the sick man, her lack of feeling at his death.

Julian himself had sometimes been something of an enigma; secretive, always turning up with surprises . . .

She opened her eyes and Lewis saw that she was looking at him.

She brought her hands to her head to smooth the scarf she had tied over her dark hair. She was no longer wearing the wedding ring, but that might be because her hands were scratched and bruised as his own were.

"You have slept well?" he asked.

"Yes." She answered him coldly. "I will relieve you now."

"No. You must sleep again."

"I have no more sleep in me."

She rose stiffly and picked up her poncho. She shook it, held it to the warmth for a moment, draped it over her shoulders, and moved to the other side of the fire as if she wished to be at a distance from him.

Most of the day she had chosen to isolate herself, but never in so marked a way as this.

She was suffering, blaming herself for their troubles and dangers. Lewis could read the thought as clearly as if she had put it down in words, and because she had been his brother's wife he wished to comfort her. Whatever she had done to Julian had not been of evil purpose. They had disagreed, no doubt. Disparity of age – she could be little more than thirty – had made adjustment difficult. They had quarrelled, perhaps, and, in ignorance of danger, she had left him in the hands of Pascual.

Lewis watched her in silence, not knowing what to say to her. She had acted to save him from Pascual, but he could only speculate about her motive. There could be no tenderness or care for him, unless she had loved Julian. It might be that there was no tenderness in her; only her pride.

He rose to put wood on the fire, and his movement seemed to startle her. She knelt and stared into the flames, and as he stood close to her, watching the play of light upon her, she covered her face, pressing her hands over her eyes.

It was a gesture of weariness, he thought. Or it was to ease the eyes still tired after the strain of the jungle. He moved away to gather more wood for the fire. When he returned he saw that she was crying.

He was distressed, and in his wish to comfort her he put a hand on her shoulder.

"Leite, what is it?"

The sort of thing that one would say to a hurt child.

He felt the shivering of her body. The draped blanket was cold to his touch. He feared that a chill of fever had gripped her and the fire could not drive it out.

On his knees beside her, he pressed upon her shoulder, drawing her towards him. The gesture was quite instinctive and her response must have been equally instinctive, an automatic yielding to the comforter.

"Leite!" In a long pause he tried to think what to say to her. "You must not give up. We'll get through to the river. I am sure of it."

"No." It was a denial of the thought behind his words. The cause of her distress was not their physical plight, but he had known this and had tried evasion.

He felt the pressure of her fingers on his arm and he desired to draw her closer, to give himself to an emotion that reason told him should be rejected. He was still a stranger to the woman; fundamentally she hated him because he was an interloper. She grasped at him only because she was in despair, unable for the moment to sustain her isolation.

"Forgive me," she said. "Please forgive me."

This time he could not misunderstand her. She was admitting her guilt in all that had happened. She waited for him to speak, but he was silent, thinking of Julian, and suddenly she drew away from him sharply. She was erect on her knees for an instant. Then she sank back, huddling under her blanket, and once more her hands covered her face.

He moved from her. He looked up at the green tangled mass of creeper that covered the wall, but he could see only a small part of the barrier. Beyond the unsteady arc of light thrown by the rise and fall of the fire was the night.

When the day came they would find a way to scale this wall. It must end somewhere, and they would follow it to its end. They would push on through the rest of the jungle till they saw the open sky again. But the other barrier, the wall between himself and the woman by the fire, was impregnable.

CHAPTER XVII

THEY STARTED AGAIN as soon as there was enough light. Pepe spun a coin and they worked to the left, which the compass said was south-south-west. They found no break in the wall, no place where they could attempt to climb. For more than a mile the obstacle continued in a straight line. Then it curved in an easterly direction.

"That's where we came from." Pepe vaguely pointed and shook his head. "If we go on much farther we'll be doubling back round the swamp." Nevertheless, they went on.

Close to the cliff the way was relatively clear. There were no thick-growing trees to impede them; only rank undergrowth, for the earth and its top covering were shallow. Like a sea that had broken upon a sunken ledge of rock, the jungle had reached a limit.

After an hour they saw clear light ahead of them, a penetration of day into the green dusk. Pepe pressed on hopefully, shouting encouragement to the others. Then he halted abruptly and stepped back with a cry of warning. They had come into the day. They saw the wide sky again, blue and cloudless, a vast cyclorama painted with the silver peaks of mountains, but before them there was nothing but space.

They stood on the edge of a precipice and a gleam of water far below showed them the depth of the ravine.

Pepe cursed the coin he had spun and led the way back to their starting point. The morning coolness had given way to heat before they saw the ashes of their fire again, but they did not pause. Now the wall ran northwards, and it seemed to go on for ever in a sheer, unbroken line.

The thought of failure was an ambush for the mind, and Lewis could avoid it only by a deliberate effort. Again he was third in line, following Leite, who kept close to Pepe. Not once did she turn to look at him. Not once in all the morning had she met his gaze or spoken a word to him.

She had withdrawn from him completely because he had turned away in the night. But now the despair was his, and he felt an insupportable weariness. He halted and closed his eyes.

When he opened them the jungle was a green spinning whorl. An arctic wind was blowing and he shivered and bent before it. His teeth were rattling with the cold and there was no strength left in him. He tried to go on, but stumbled and fell.

"Leite!"

He called her name with all the breath that he had left, but he knew the result was a feeble whisper that could not reach her, for she was far ahead, keeping up with the urgent Pepe. When he raised himself to look, she was out of sight.

Half hidden by fern fronds and lush grass, he lay in a shivering torment. He tried to reach his rolled poncho, thinking of its blanket warmth, but it had fallen too far from him and he was too weak to crawl to it. He closed his eyes again and he felt better. He felt quite normal and comfortable.

In a minute or two his plane would be landing at Santa Teresa. He had longed all the way from London for the journey's end, but now he did not want it. He would not care if he went on and on, down to Valparaiso and farther so long as he could look at the woman across the aisle. If only he could meet her, there might be a new beginning to life. But inexorably the plane would land at Santa Teresa, and he would never see her again.

"Lewis!"

She was calling his name and her hand was on his brow.

He looked up with an effort and saw the dark eyes full of concern for him. And Pepe was bending down, peering over her shoulder.

"Lewis! What happened? Have you hurt yourself?"

He tried to tell her that the plane must have crashed. He felt little pain, only the ache of his broken bones. Every bone in his body.

She wiped his brow and put her hand on him again. Then she rose and looked at Pepe.

"All the demons!" Pepe swore. "Even this has to happen."

"There's quinine in the food pack. Get it for me. Bring the brown box."

Before he returned she had the ponchos spread over Lewis.

"Now go ahead on your own," she ordered Pepe. "I'll wait here till you have found a place where we can climb."

"How will he climb with malaria?"

"How do we know that it is malaria? Don't stand there like that. Give me the water-bag and get on with the search. I will get him on to his feet somehow."

She raised Lewis with an arm round his shoulders. She made him swallow two tablets and drink some water. Then she pulled the blankets over him and bade him rest.

He was saying something about Julian. It did not matter about Julian any longer. All he wished for was that she should forgive him.

"Sleep," she urged him. "Try to sleep."

She stood up and stared with aching eyes at the wall. There were always barriers to doing and living. They rose out of self-delusion, credulity, hatred, fanaticism. Illusions closed your eyes to the realities round you.

"You are a fool, Leite," Maria Josefa had croaked at her. "You trick yourself into the belief that you have a duty to perform. You have a duty to yourself: to forget San Mateo and live."

"How can you be so indifferent?"

"I am old and have grown wise. Between the Bartols and the Recaldes there is no choice. They are all of the kind who spat on Bolivar when he lay dying. Do you think that Pascual is another Liberator? He is a self-seeking rogue, and Bartol is an imbecile to trust him."

"He is an instrument."

"Of what? Divine Providence? You will tell me next that you hear voices, like Joan of Arc. The only voice you hear comes from a devil in you. Your one passion is hatred."

"Bartol will restore the name of my father. He will give us back our property."

"A heap of ruins in a wilderness."

"Is it wrong to wish for justice?"

"What you are doing is wrong. Your motive is as selfish as Pascual's, and he will commit you to his own evil ways. Come away with me before it is too late."

It was too late. The wall reached higher than the green roof of the jungle, but there were omens in her path more formidable. It would always matter about Julian Page.

Lewis was sleeping. She stooped to feel his head again and she was sure that the abnormal heat had passed. She sat beside him and watched. She had conceived of his salvation as a debt to be discharged, an expiation, but this was only part of the truth. It did not explain the sudden impulse to join him on this mad flight or the transformation of a matter of conscience into an intense personal desire to secure his safety.

She stood up again and peered into the green shadows along the wall. The jungle was full of noise. Through the chattering and screeching and droning came a sound that was like laughter; the high treble laughter of an animal.

Then suddenly, as if by a command, all the noise ceased except the droning and rustle of the insects.

The loneliness was terrifying. She looked back at Lewis, but no wave of sympathy could come from him.

If he died . . . If Pepe were lost . . .

Panic was waiting for her. She wanted to call to Pepe, though she knew he must be far beyond hearing.

It seemed an interminable time since he had gone. Certainly it must have been more than an hour, and now her anxiety increased with each minute. She went along the path he had made through the undergrowth, hoping to meet him, but she was afraid to go far.

When she returned, Lewis had thrown the blankets aside and was sitting up.

"Keep the covers over you," she bade him urgently.

"I'm all right," he told her. "A bit shaky. That's all."

He moved to rise, but she pushed him back firmly and piled the blankets on him again. "You must stay where you are," she said. "We can do nothing till Pepe returns."

Once more she felt his brow. She was relieved. She searched among the drugs in the brown box and made him swallow another tablet. It seemed that the chill was not serious. No doubt the real trouble was exhaustion.

The time of waiting dragged on, but at last Pepe returned and his excitement was obvious at a distance. He shouted his news before he reached them.

"I have found a gap. At least we have a chance, if Don Lewis can climb."

"First we will eat," she answered. "That will allow him to rest a little longer."

"Good." Pepe resumed command. "We shall have to leave most things behind with our ponchos. We can pick them up again if we have to come back."

After they had eaten they selected the articles they must take: the water-bag, some food, the revolver, the machetes, the straps from the ponchos, the brown box. Then Lewis was given another tablet and Leite, as though he were still without strength, helped him to rise.

She was apprehensive, feeling the trembling of his hand in hers, but he insisted that he was well enough to go forward. She watched him, keeping close to him as they moved off, and her anxiety was not allayed till Pepe had brought them to his discovery.

A landslide in some remote time had broken the cliff, leaving a moraine-like ramp of debris. How high it would take them they could not tell, for the top of the slope was masked by a dense mass of vegetation.

They climbed slowly and painfully, and frequently they fell forward as the rotten rock under the tangle of creeper slid from their feet. The smooth-worn rock was wet and slippery and kept from packing down by an oozing of water from a small stream that found a bed somewhere beneath the surface rubble; but if the foothold was uncertain, the creeper at least offered an advantage, for it secured them from sliding back down the slope.

A faint sound of falling water reached them from far above, possibly from a rivulet fed by the mountain snows. The rubble was icy to the touch and leather soles were no protection from the chill of it.

After they had toiled abreast for a half hour, concern for Lewis made Pepe call for a brief halt. Lewis objected. The angle of the ramp was helping him, for he was constantly steadied by his hands in the upward crawl. He felt a little dizzy when he straightened himself, but protested that he could go on.

Leite insisted on the rest. Although Lewis was doing well enough, taking energy from the drug she had given him, she feared the inevitable reaction would bring a worse exhaustion and a recurrence of his fever.

When they went on they were not far from the screen of vegetation they had seen from the jungle floor, and now the sound of falling water increased with each yard that they gained. At last they caught a glimpse of sky and were spurred on by the hope that they might be close to the summit.

Certainly they were near the top of the ramp. The rubble ended, and they clambered over a sharp-edged step of rock to find themselves in a thick shrubbery of ferns and saplings. They pushed and thrust forward, hacking when necessary, but the path laboriously made led to disappointment. They had gained only a wide ledge. Another wall was before them.

Bitter discouragement drew exclamations from Lewis and Leite. Pepe was silent, looking up, measuring the further obstacle. A few yards to the right a stream fell from a height of twenty feet or more into a dark pool. Pepe tasted the water.

"It is good," he said. "We can fill our bag."

They drank. They had been very sparing with their water but had come near to the end of it.

"We will eat a little, too," Pepe announced. "Then we climb. This wall is not so high. It is broken and we have the stream to guide us.

Fortunately we brought the straps. We will need them."

He was particular about the period of respite. Now, if ever, they would have need of their second wind, but he took little rest himself. He examined the wall, he buckled the straps together to form a line, he took off his worn boots and secured them by the laces so that he could sling them over a shoulder.

"You will need your good soles," he said. "My feet are hard. I will go first and haul you after me."

There were moments in the climb that would bring nausea to Lewis whenever he recalled them. Waiting on a narrow step while Leite was using the strap-line, the ague attacked him again.

"Don't look down," Pepe had urged more than once, but Lewis had looked down. Then the cliff seemed to be tipping over, spilling him into space. He clawed at the rock and somehow managed to cling on.

After that Leite demanded that he should always go up before her.

There was another moment when a foothold crumbled under her and she hung from the strap, but Pepe had been ready to take the first shock of it, and Lewis helped him to draw her to safety.

Step after giant step the stream took its plunging way down a deep ravine with steep unscalable sides, and step after step the climbers pushed their advance, till at last they lay exhausted at the top.

There was thick timber ahead, but sky was over them, and when they started again they realised that the way was downhill.

"We are near the end," Pepe said.

He was right.

They emerged on the brow of a hill, and at the bottom of a wide valley they saw the sheen of the river that rolled sluggishly on its curving course.

Far to the north, through an opening in the hills, Lewis gazed upon a hazy patch of blue and knew it was the Pacific.

The sun was low over the westward heights. Lewis observed it and turned again to the north.

By now the *Atacama* would be through the Canal and speeding southward from Balboa, and to-morrow would be Anne's last day at sea. Some time on the following morning the ship would dock at

Santa Teresa.

If he could reach Trajano to-night, he would be in plenty of time for to-morrow's plane to the port. But he was no longer anxious. If he missed the plane, he could wire to Anne to go to the Hotel Granada and wait for him.

A paddle-wheeler towing a long raft moved down the river, but it would be days before it reached the port.

The only quick route was the plane from Trajano, and the problem now was to get to Trajano.

Pepe was already trudging down the hill.

"Come on," he called. "If we have any luck, someone on the road will give us a lift."

He was a long way ahead when they neared the road.

A distant hoot from the paddle-wheeler's siren reached Lewis through a confusion of noise that had started in his head.

He closed his eyes, but then the noise was worse. He tried to hide from Leite the fact that he was shivering. He lurched, and her hand was at his elbow to steady him.

Pepe had passed out of sight into a narrow belt of scrub lower down the slope. Lewis struggled on with Leite supporting him. The noise in his head had dimmed down to a summer buzz of insects. It was still troublesome, but he was alert. He could see clearly. The difficulty was that he had little control over his limbs.

He reached the belt of scrub, but the farther edge of it brought him to the end of endurance. He sank down on his knees in the tall grass, and Leite was beside him, holding him with an arm round him.

"It's all right now," she said. "There is a truck on the road. Pepe will stop it. We'll soon reach Trajano."

He saw the truck moving slowly along the road, very slowly, as if it were going nowhere in particular. Pepe was running down the hill, shouting. The truck pulled up and a number of men sprang from its hooded interior and fanned out in the roadway.

Pepe halted as though he had crashed into an invisible barrier. Next, he wheeled and started up the hill again like a frightened rabbit. There was a crack-crack of rifle fire, and Lewis saw that the men from the truck were pausing to shoot as they came on, still fanning out.

A bullet whanged through the scrub, passing very close. Pepe threw himself down behind a boulder.

Then he had his revolver in hand and was returning the fire.

The men came on steadily, surely, and Pepe had no bullets left. He was on his feet again and running for the scrub. He was half-way across the open space when he leaped high, twisted sideways, and crashed to the ground.

Leite's hands gripped Lewis under the arms and she dragged him back into the deeper cover of the scrub.

The men with the rifles came on.

CHAPTER XVIII

THERE WERE bright stars that night when you looked out from the bows of the *Atacama*. Anne tried to find the Southern Cross, but so many cruciform patterns appeared in the sky that she could never be certain about it. The third officer had pointed it out to her, Don Sebastian had pointed it out; only Del Wayne had not bothered.

Probably Del Wayne knew nothing about stars, or he had other things to think of. Since the day in Havana he had been moody and preoccupied, seeming to come out of himself only when he snarled at Don Sebastian.

"Star-gazing?" Don Sebastian inquired. "You will find nothing up there to equal your eyes."

Compliments from Don Sebastian had become irritating.

"I think that's a very silly thing to say," she snapped at him.

"That is because you do not see yourself." He was quite undisturbed. "You are very lovely to-night, Anne. And in a different way. What has made such a change in you?"

Carmen had persuaded her to do her hair in a new way. Carmen had insisted on a different lipstick. Perhaps, under Carmen's tutelage, she had rather overdone it.

Sebastian's elbow touched hers on the rail. He was good at that sort of thing.

"What a pity there is no dancing to-night," he lamented. "But to-morrow, our last night at sea, you will dance with me again?"

"I might."

"The last night," Don Sebastian sighed. "I cannot bear to think that we must part so soon."

111

His hand caressed her shoulder and would have stayed there had she not turned abruptly from the rail.

"We must part this very moment," she said. "I have to get a message off to Santa Teresa."

"You leave me in desolation."

"You had better take Carmen to the film. She wants to see it."

She ran to her cabin and peered into the mirror. The lipstick was all right, but the general effect did not satisfy her. She worked on it for several minutes, then stared at herself.

Don Sebastian was right. She was changed, but the transformation went deeper than he imagined.

When had she ever borrowed an iron to press a dress? When had she ever consulted a Spanish dancer about the right shade of lipstick? When, indeed, had she ever cared a button for cosmetics or brushed her hair so carefully? Or, for that matter, when had she ever rushed from a ship's cabin to keep a date with a copper-miner?

"Why have you been so long?" the copper-miner grumbled.

"I like that," she retorted. "I waited where you said till I was tired of waiting."

"I'm sorry. Sparks was chasing me with a radio. I had to get a reply off. I'm having a row with the dad."

"By wireless?"

"That's how we always have our rows. It saves his blood pressure. Only this time I doubt if it will. He's not going to dictate to me any more. I've sent him an ultimatum."

"But, Del, you make it sound quite serious."

"It is serious. Now forget it. Let's have coffee in the lounge."

"Must we? I don't feel dressed for a crowd."

"You'll pass. Why do you have to use that lipstick? You don't need it."

She looked at him reproachfully, then shrank from the amusement in his eyes, embarrassed by the thought of how crudely she had angled for a compliment. Her reproach was now for herself, and when she was once more in her cabin she stared at the image in the mirror with distaste.

It was the sea voyage, of course. Sea voyages did strange things to people. Carmen had told her that, rather cryptically, and it was true. She was no longer the Anne Page who had embarked at New York, the serious artist, looking forward to days of work on her string quartet. Alas, the string quartet was forgotten; so, too, was the choral opus, "Where the remote Bermudas ride."

Since Havana she had thought of nothing but dressing up and dancing and sight-seeing, of shuffleboard and deck tennis: all the trivial pursuits of the empty-headed.

Worry over the creature she had become kept her awake, and in the small hours she framed resolutions of reform. There was one day left to dissipate the effects of the voyage. To-morrow she would retrieve herself.

She began the day by hurling her lipstick through the port-hole, but she dressed without diminution of her newly-acquired care. This was no compromise; it was merely to preserve certain desirable aspects of the sea change. There was no need for a sane and serious composer to be a slovenly frump.

At the last minute, just as the steward came along thumping the breakfast gong, she thought of Uncle Julian's ring. As she would have to wear it to-morrow, it would be well to give it an airing.

Don Sebastian, of course, was the first to notice it. He reached across the table and caught her hand in his long and elegant fingers, and Del Wayne glared at her disapprovingly as if she were encouraging the man.

"What a beautiful ring, Anne!" Don Sebastian exclaimed. "Why is it that you have not worn it before?"

Anne explained. Don Sebastian squeezed her hand.

"Cantaloup," Delbert snarled at the steward. "And see that it's properly iced."

Don Sebastian said: "May I examine the stone, please?"

"I don't think it's a very good one." Anne slipped the ring from her finger and handed it over.

"But it is a good one." Don Sebastian peered at it, held it to the light, turned it to examine the facets. "I know all about emeralds," he added modestly. "Before I discovered my voice, I worked in our Mines Department. My cousin is the Minister."

"You seem to come of a very powerful family," Delbert said unpleasantly.

"In San Mateo it is good to come of a powerful family." Don Sebastian bent over the ring. "The setting is perfect, Anne, but I hope you will pardon me if I say the stone could have been better cut."

Delbert jerked his head back. "I don't see why you have to disturb Miss Page with your damn-fool criticisms.

"I'm not in the least disturbed." Miss Page turned a reproving eye on her protector. "The ring has a sentimental value. That's all."

"Accept my apologies." Don Sebastian was contrite. "The expert in me made me forget myself. We take great pride in the craft of our cutters. Even a small fault is to be deplored. It involves the honour of my cousin's department."

"Your cousin's department is quite safe." Anne laughed. "The stone was cut and set in London."

"But that is impossible!" Don Sebastian was really surprised. "You say it came from San Mateo. In San Mateo emeralds are a government monopoly. No stone is permitted to leave the country uncut. It is the law." He frowned, quite puzzled. "It is also the law that no one may sell an uncut stone."

"I'm afraid my uncle couldn't have known about it. Anyway, he didn't buy the emerald. He found it on his estate. He certainly didn't think it had any value."

"Where is his estate?"

Del was suddenly in a good humour. "Careful, Anne, or you'll find the whole family under arrest. Your uncle is obviously a notorious jewel smuggler."

Sebastian flushed angrily. "You like to be absurd, señor. Miss Page understands that I am interested merely in the source of the stone."

Del's good humour passed in a flash. He bristled. "I don't see what business it is of yours!"

"Please!" Anne interposed, holding out her hand for the ring.

People at nearby tables were staring. Sebastian continued to glare, but before he could frame an indignant retort, Carmen appeared and demanded attention.

"Sebastian!" she cried in the voice of a Cassandra. "Have you seen this?"

Her dark eyes had the fear of ruin in them as she thrust the daily news sheet at him.

"What is it now?" he asked, turning some of his rancour upon her.

"There has been shooting," Carmen announced tragically. "Read!"
Sebastian read.

"Why must you always get so excited over nothing?" he demanded. "A river steamer reports hearing a few shots in the hills north-east of Trajano!"

"But it happened only yesterday afternoon!"

"So! It may happen again this afternoon. There are always hunting parties in those hills. I have given you my word that there will be no insurrection. Now sit down, and see that you do not eat too much. If you put on weight, you will spoil the season."

Del rose, grinning. "I'll see you later, Anne," he said. "I have to get through a pile of papers to catch the air-mail to New York to-morrow. I'll be on deck as soon as possible."

When she passed his cabin at lunch-time, she heard the furious clicking of a typewriter, and his steward was coming along the alleyway with a sandwich and a glass of milk.

It was late in the afternoon before he came to his deck-chair. He seemed tired and nervous and resentful of the presence of Carmen and Sebastian. He tried to detach Anne from the party, but the other two defeated him, so they were a foursome till they broke up to dress for dinner.

Anne had pressed her once-despised ball creation for this last night, and she thought it would be too absurd to crush it into a suitcase again after all her hard work with Carmen's portable iron.

Perhaps, as a reformed character, she hesitated for a moment. Then she put it on. It was an airy, delicate thing of white tulle and miniature pink roses, and it gave her a deplorable feeling of self-satisfaction.

To make up for it she devoted a few spare minutes to the "Principles of Orchestration", but it seemed that Rimsky-Korsakov had lost his charm. Properly distributed chords had no interest for her, and it was boring to think how they might sound in strings, woodwind or brass. She wished she had accepted Don Sebastian's invitation to a cocktail in the bar. She wanted to hear how the human voice would respond to her symphony of tulle and roses.

The response, when she went to dinner, was mainly in the husky folk-contralto of Carmen. The tenor of Don Sebastian could not get beyond the utterance of her name, but his eyes were eloquent. She turned nervously towards Del, but, for all the notice he took, she might have been wearing her old blue jeans and a crumpled shirt.

Sebastian insisted on champagne. "We must celebrate our last night," he said. "It is nice to know that Anne will be with us in San Mateo. To poor old Del we must soon say good-bye, but we will think of him as he sails down to Antofagasta."

Poor old Del was not happy. He was thinking too much of Antofagasta. Or he was worried about the quarrel with his dad.

Towards the end of the meal the table steward brought him a message.

"From the wireless officer, sir."

Scowling, Del read the message, then laughed and thrust it into a pocket of his jacket.

"Damned old fool!" he exclaimed involuntarily, and called for more champagne.

When the time came for dancing Anne completely forgot her reformation. A languorous tango was heavenly music, and there could surely be no one to better Don Sebastian as a partner. The only trouble with him was that he would talk a lot of nonsense.

She tried to laugh it off, but he became more and more insistent. They must make a plan. He would meet her in Trajano, and the town would be hers. She must come to the opera and he would sing to her. Only to her.

When he drew her closer, she wanted to escape. She looked towards Del Wayne as they moved past him, but he merely scowled at her. The tango came to an end and Sebastian still held her.

"The next dance," he pleaded.

"Sorry," she answered. "It's promised."

Del said: "Let's sit this one out."

The proprietary note in his voice made her frown. He seemed to think he could order her about whenever the mood took him. She wanted to rebel, yet she followed him to the deserted promenade. Tamely. Or tamed. Suddenly she halted.

"I promised you the dance," she protested hotly. "Why do you think you can cart me off down here?"

He was insensitive to her temper. Like Sebastian, he could think only of himself. He hauled the crumpled wireless message from his pocket and thrust it at her.

"Take a look at this."

She faltered. Her anger evaporated.

"Is it from your father?" she asked.

"Read it!"

He was tense, watching her closely. She took a step towards a deck light and read:

BEG YOU COME TO   YOUR SENSES STOP HATE SEE YOU
VICTIMISED BY ADVENTURESS STOP AUTHORISE YOU BUY HER
OFF STOP WILL MEET ANY REASONABLE SUM AVOID BREACH
ACTION STOP THIS IS MY LAST WORD STOP IF YOU MARRY HER
EXPECT NOTHING FROM ME REPEAT NOTHING

She was sinking, as if the ship had foundered beneath her. She tried to tell herself that it did not matter to her. He could have a dozen adventuresses waiting for him in Antofagasta for all she cared.

Yet she continued to sink, and she had a choking sensation as if the sea had closed over her. And he was standing there watching her, waiting for her to say something.

"Why do you show this to me?" She stared at the slip of paper and saw that her hand was trembling. "Are you going to marry this – this woman?" she asked in a faint voice.

"It depends on you."

"How can it depend on me? What have I to do with it?"

She looked up to find him pulling nervously at his collar.

"You happen to be the woman," he said.

She was rising to the surface and his hands reached out to pull her to safety.

It was a long time before a disquieting thought came to her.

"What about your father?" she asked.

"Please don't worry about him," Del advised her. "My bet is that you'll have him under control in thirty seconds. Of course, we could get him to buy you off. Then we could marry on the proceeds. An adventuress with your looks should be worth a million at least. Let's go to the captain and make him marry us right away."

"Don't be absurd. You'll meet my father in Santa Teresa to-morrow. Then we'll talk about it."

But they talked about it until well after midnight, and they had plans worked out to the last detail before they parted.

Next morning they stood by the rail in silence, watching the coastline of San Mateo coming up out of the haze with hateful rapidity. They were solemn, even grim, for the landfall was ominous with the threat of the imminent parting.

The deck-steward came along with the kind of envelope that was only too familiar to one of the dejected couple. Del held out a hand to take it.

"For Miss Page," the deck-steward told him.

"This time it will be from my father," Anne said as she broke the envelope. Then her look changed from one of expectancy to alarm. "Del! He's ill."

Del read the message:

SORRY CANNOT MEET SHIP DOWN WITH TOUCH OF FEVER NOTHING SERIOUS AM SENDING FRIEND WITH TAXI AWAIT YOU AT HOTEL LOVE

"He says it isn't serious," Del comforted her. "What shall we do about to-day?"

She frowned. "He'll surely be well enough to see you, even if it's only for a moment. Del, he must see you."

"I had better go along with you as soon as we dock."

"No. I must prepare him. I'm afraid it will be a bit of a shock. You come to the Hotel Granada at one. Whatever happens, we'll have four hours together before the ship sails."

She read the message again. "It's funny that he has to send a friend with a taxi," she remarked. "I would have thought that Uncle Julian would meet me."

"Perhaps he was too busy to make the trip. Anyway, you'll all be together very soon. And I'll be back here before you have time to miss me."

Details of the Santa Teresa waterfront were already distinguishable, and presently a launch came alongside with the medical and immigration officers. A few minutes later Anne was summoned to the saloon to join a queue of disembarking passengers and Del went in search of expected letters.

The *Atacama* docked at eleven. In the last few minutes of bustle with mooring ropes and gangways, Don Sebastian waylaid Anne.

"I had hoped to take you ashore, but my people are meeting me," he told her. "Where can I get in touch with you?"

"I don't know." She looked for Del, but he was nowhere in sight. "I'll write to the Opera House," she added hastily.

"Do that." Don Sebastian was delighted. "I'll be keeping a box for you every night. I must rush away now. *Au revoir,* my dear. *Hasta la vista.* "

He kissed her hand.

"*Adios,*" she said.

"No, no! *Hasta la vista.* "

At last Del came pushing through the crush of passengers round the gangway.

"I was kept at the purser's office," he complained, flourishing a handful of letters. "Now there's urgent mail to deal with, but I'll be on time if I have to drop everything. Where's your escort?"

"I don't know." She glanced up and down and across the deck, then laughed at the futility of it. "I suppose he'll ask someone to find me. If he doesn't turn up, I can take a taxi."

People were coming and going, greeting friends, calling names. She felt helpless in all the confusion. Then she saw the deck-steward pointing her out to a man in a chauffeur's cap. The man came forward.

"Pardon," he said. "You are Señorita Page, yes? Your friend waits for you in my cab. I have orders to help with your baggage."

He was a spindly specimen with a large protruding nose and a receding chin.

"Where is your cab?" Del demanded.

"On the Embarcadero, señor. It is not permitted on the pier. If the young lady hurries, we will get through the Customs quickly."

"Lead the way."

"I'm all right now, Del," Anne protested. "You get on with your letters."

"Do you think I'm going to let you out of my sight till the last second?" He took her arm. "I'll see you safely to your cab."

The taxi-driver was efficient. He found Anne's suitcases, caught the attention of a Customs officer, and argued with such urgency that the formalities were completed in little more than a minute.

Del was stopped at the exit. It seemed that his blue permit had to be presented at another gate. This one was strictly for pink disembarkation cards. A display of pesos had no effect, so he could only watch from inside the barrier while Anne followed the driver across the roadway.

On the far side of the taxi-cab a distinguished-looking gentleman awaited her. He was tall and thin and the length of his lean sun-browned face was accentuated by a greying goatee. He wore his immaculate clothes with an aristocrat's ease, and he bowed most elegantly.

"I am charmed, Miss Page," he said. "I trust you were not too disturbed by your father's message?"

"Not greatly, thank you, señor." Anne was quite shy in the presence.

"That is good. He is, I may say, much better this morning. Much, much better. But it is unwise for him to leave his room for a day or so.

If you will permit me, I will take you to him at once."

"You are very kind, señor."

"It is nothing, señorita." The stranger smiled. "I have had the pleasure to serve your father before to-day. My name is Balaguer. Mauricio Balaguer y Lucientes."

CHAPTER XIX

THE RECEPTIONIST asserted that no one named Page had registered at the Hotel Granada.

"Page," Del repeated, trying a Spanish pronunciation. "Señor Lewis Page and his daughter Anna?"

"I understand perfectly, señor." The receptionist was patient. "We have no one of that name."

"But it is not possible!" Del stared at the clerk in growing dismay. "Señorita Page arrived by the *Atacama* less than two hours ago."

"I assure you, señor." The receptionist shrugged.

"Possibly the reservations are in the name of Julian Page?"

"I am sorry, señor. I cannot help you."

Del looked round the foyer, but there was no sign of Anne. "Perhaps a message has been left for me," he suggested, and gave his name.

"Not at this desk, señor, but I will inquire."

Observing the young man's distress, the receptionist was sympathetic. He touched a bell, but the head porter could only shake his head. Del described Anne and the dress she was wearing. The porter looked at the receptionist and they both shrugged helplessly, the gesture implying that they would have produced a half-dozen Annes if they had had the power.

Del was moving away in bewilderment when the receptionist called him back.

"One moment, señor." He turned the leaves of his register. "Ah, yes. I thought the name was familiar. We had a Señor Page here on the seventh of this month. He stayed one night and left by the plane for Trajano next day."

"Yes, that's the man," Del agreed hopefully.

"We have had no application from him since. Perhaps he has gone to one of the other hotels. I might suggest that you try the España. I will telephone, if you wish."

"Thanks. I'll go round."

Del took hope again. The message from Anne's father had not named the hotel. Anne had assumed it to be the Granada, but there may have been a change of plan.

He tried the España. Then he went on to the remainder of the feasible hotels and his search became more and more a panic action. He returned to the Granada to ask if any message had come in for him since his first visit. The receptionist looked into the anxious eyes of the young man and shook his head slowly.

"Surely it is just an unfortunate mistake, señor," he argued. "In time you will hear from your friend."

"In time?" Del looked at his watch. "My ship sails in an hour."

"I have been thinking. The air line put on an extra flight to Trajano to-day for some important passengers from the *Atacama*. Perhaps your friends were in a hurry to reach the capital and managed to get seats."

"But Señorita Page would have let me know."

"Is it possible that she sent a message to the ship? In the event of a sudden change . . ."

Del cut him short with a word of thanks and dashed for his waiting taxi. In his desperation he was ready to follow any gleam of hope without pausing to consider the probabilities.

He reached the *Atacama* in a matter of minutes, only to find that no message had been received for him.

"Is there a telephone line to the shore?" he demanded.

There was.

He called up the airport. No one named Page had travelled by the extra plane. It had been reserved strictly for the party of the Minister of Fine Arts, Dr. Byrne, and his son, the famous tenor.

Sebastian!

But the thought and its implications were not to be entertained for a moment. Anne was incapable of duplicity.

There was only one thing left to do, and he might have done it much earlier, if only it had occurred to him.

The name was there, in the Trajano Directory: Page, J., Casa Alta, Rosario 24.

He had to wait twenty minutes before the call could be put through. He asked for Señor Julian Page.

"What is your business with Señor Page?" the voice at the other end of the line inquired.

"I will explain that to him." Del spoke sharply, moved by his urgency. "It's personal," he added. "I'm a friend."

"Can I do anything for you? I am the estate manager."

"Listen! My ship is sailing in a few minutes. I must speak to Señor Page."

"Your ship? I see." A moment of hesitation, and the voice went on. "I am afraid that you have not heard the sad news. Señor Page died last week."

"Died? But . . ." Del tightened his grip on the receiver. "How can I get in touch with his brother, Lewis Page? Where is he staying in Santa Teresa?"

"I don't understand, señor. If you will explain your business, I will try to help. You are an American buyer of our coffee?"

"I have nothing to do with coffee. I'm on my way to Chile. Please tell me where I can find Lewis Page."

"There seems to be some mistake, señor. I know of no one named Lewis Page."

"But he has been staying with you at the Casa Alta."

"No, señor. We have had no guests."

Del stared at the dead telephone for quite two minutes. Then he made up his mind.

"I'm making a stop-over," he told the purser. "Please get my baggage through to our agent at Antofagasta. I'll pack a suitcase."

"But, Mr. Wayne, we're sailing in seven minutes!"

"It will take me three. The officials are still on the dock, aren't they?"

A half-hour later he had left his suitcase at the Granada and was on his way to police headquarters, heavy with despair as thoughts of all he had read or heard of crime and white slave traffic ran in his mind. He had discounted the worst stories as exaggerations or as feasible only under conditions that had been cleaned up, but now, in his disturbed vision, every road led to Buenos Aires.

Frantic as he was, he realised the importance of establishing his identity as a means of securing action.

He gave his name to a dubious-eyed official. He added: "I'm the son of Beckett Wayne of Wayne Copper Mines Incorporated, New York and Antofagasta."

Everyone in South America knew Beckett Wayne, if only for his eccentricities.

The official jerked to a more respectful attitude, excused himself, and returned in a moment to announce that Inspector Chavez would see Mr. Wayne.

Inspector Chavez was small, thin and tired. He looked like one who has been permanently cheated of his siesta. When his eyes threw off their sleepiness, they took on a satirical glint.

"What can I do for you, Mr. Wayne?" he inquired in precisely enunciated English.

Mr. Wayne told the whole story of his day in full detail. He lingered over his description of the taxi-driver who had boarded the ship, for this man had become the first suspect in his mind and the sallow face with the long nose and the receding chin had acquired a sinister cast.

Chavez turned to the window, wishing, perhaps, to hide the satirical glint in his eyes.

"Have you not thought, señor, that you may be alarming yourself unnecessarily?" he asked.

"I'm telling you the girl has disappeared, vanished. She stepped into this taxi, and no one has seen her since."

"No one?" Chavez faced his earnest young visitor. With the glint controlled, his eyes expressed only a professional suspicion of the world in general. "It is rather a large assumption that the father did not see her, and she was no doubt under the observation of the friend who met her. Unquestionably a trusted friend, since the father arranged it.

You saw him, señor?"

"I saw a figure behind the cab, vaguely. Why did he hide himself behind the cab?"

"Since, as you say, he was waiting on the pavement, he was naturally obscured by the body of the cab."

"Listen, Inspector! Lewis Page came from London to visit his brother. They say at the Casa Alta that they know nothing about him. The brother dies, and no word is sent to Miss Page. Doesn't it occur to you that there is something very queer about this?"

"You have a theory?"

"Yes, I have. A gang of some sort is holding Lewis Page. The same gang has kidnapped his daughter."

"All this because you did not find the daughter at the Hotel Granada?" Chavez gave up trying to hide the glint. The young man was rather amusing. A romantic might have shown him commiseration, he was so patently the victim of a shipboard coquette, but romance had died in Chavez with the birth of his seventh girl and the issue of the latest promotion list.

"Mr. Wayne," he said, "what do you really know about this Miss Page and her father?"

Mr. Wayne glared. He was becoming more and more the son of his bulldozing dad. The old scoundrel might cut him off without a penny, but there was a legacy that could not be cancelled.

"Miss Page and I are engaged to be married," Mr. Wayne snapped.

"With the consent of Mr. Page?"

"I have already told you I was to have met Mr. Page for the first time."

"That is what I have in mind." The inspector's patient mildness expressed deprecation of the young man's violent tone. "Also," he added, "I am not forgetting that you met the young lady for the first time on this voyage from New York."

In effect he was saying: "We all know these shipboard flirtations. For a young girl on a holiday, a sea trip is dull without them."

Del came into his full inheritance. "Goddam it!" he roared. "Haven't I given you enough of a case?"

"A view, rather than a case, sir."

"Look here, Inspector Chavez, or whatever your name is, I want you to know clearly −"

The inspector held up a beautifully manicured hand. At the same time his jaw developed a certain pugnacity.

"If you are about to imply that you are the son of Beckett Wayne, I assure you I have already taken the point."

The hand came down and went quickly to a concealed bell-push between the pedestals of the desk.

"My department will do its best to trace this Englishman and his daughter," Chavez said. "I suggest that you return to the Hotel Granada and wait till you hear from me. Above all, I recommend that you cease to play the detective."

Del went back to the Granada with a new sense of frustration weighting his despair. He was convinced that Chavez looked on the whole thing as a harmless comedy and would do nothing. And there was nothing more he could do himself. For all the help he was able to bring to Anne, he might as well be back in the *Atacama,* speeding down the coast to the next port of call.

Wearily he recalled that he had an obligation to discharge. He wrote a telegram to Antofagasta to say that he was detained in Santa Teresa and would come on by plane as soon as possible. His message to the authority in New York was more personal. The only information it gave was that he had jumped ship and was remaining in San Mateo indefinitely.

Back at headquarters, Chavez was in consultation with his chief.

"I don't like it," he complained. "I find it is quite true that this Julian Page died last week. It is also true that the manager at the finca knows nothing of a brother, let alone a brother's daughter. At least, that is what he claims. Unfortunately the widow is not available. Prostrated by grief, she has left the estate temporarily."

The chief frowned heavily. "You think this Lewis Page and the daughter are impostors?"

"I think only of the time when Beckett Wayne was kidnapped and held for ransom."

"But that was in Chile. This is San Mateo."

Chavez ignored the irrelevance. "That, too, began on a voyage. The trap, you may remember, was baited with a Bolivian actress."

"Some of these Bolivians are handsome women," the chief sighed.

"What has that to do with it?"

"Eh?" The chief came out of his momentary dream and was all sagacity. "It points to variations, doesn't it?"

"Each case has its variations."

"That's what I mean." Thought furrowed the chief's wide brow. "If this pseudo-English girl was being used as a lure, why is it that she and her supposed father vanish at the moment when the trap should have closed? And why, in the name of all the demons, should the girl claim relationship with an actual English planter in the wilds of Rosario?"

"Verisimilitude," Chavez murmured. "A girl, travelling alone and without a feasible identity, would be suspect."

"So she picks on this obscure Englishman?"

"The obscure Englishman is internationally known as an archaeologist."

"Absurd, Chavez! Is young Wayne interested in archaeology? No! Like his lamentable father, he inclines to biology. The study of the young female."

"He has not that reputation. He impressed me as being an eminently sincere young man."

"What impresses me is that nothing makes sense."

"Thirty years have I laboured in this vineyard," Chavez sighed. "Never have the grapes ripened according to the laws of agronomics."

"Where do grapes come into it?" the chief demanded.

"Nowhere, if you put it like that," Chavez admitted with another and different sigh. "Perhaps the plotters have developed a more subtle technique. Phase one: the innocence of the lure is established by the clever use of verisimilitude."

"Let us dispense with verisimilitude," the chief pleaded.

"Phase two: the victim is induced to break his voyage. Phase three: contact —"

"Phase four, five, six!" the chief roared. "If young Wayne is kidnapped, there will be no grapes. The inferno will break loose, as it did in Chile."

"But this is San Mateo. Young Wayne will not be kidnapped. I have advised him that he must stay in the Hotel Granada till he hears from me."

"You have advised him! Chavez, I can see only further disappointment for you when the next promotion list comes out. Do you think this fool Americano will heed your advice?"

"I have taken other measures," Chavez said modestly.

CHAPTER XX

FOR TWO HOURS the fool Americano waited in the Granada. Then he conceived the idea of searching for the sinister taxi-driver.

Santa Teresa was not a large town. The chances of success were considerably more than would be offered by a pin in a cornfield, and Del proceeded methodically, aided by a street plan on which the head porter had marked the positions of the main cab-ranks.

He went on foot at first so that he might examine the features of the driver of any passing or waiting cab. There were several vehicles on the Plaza rank and they yielded taxi-men with sallow faces, others with long noses, and at least two with receding chins, but none with the looked-for combination.

Disappointed, he trudged on to the railway terminus and here again he had no luck, though there was quite an assembly of vehicles waiting for the train from Trajano. Some of the drivers sat somnolently in their seats. Others, gathered in a knot, were engaged in a violent political argument.

Del broke in on them. He claimed to have left a cigarette-case in a taxi and proceeded to a description of his man.

"Of a certainty that is Pedro the Camel," one of the group asserted.

"No, no," another objected. "It is Antonio Ruiz."

"You are wrong," a third insisted. "It is Jean the Frenchman. He has the biggest nose in the business."

"Where did you pick up the cab? At the pier? Then you should look along the Embarcadero. José Fernandez is the man you want. Next time you should take the number."

Del hired one of them on the assurance that José could readily be found. Argument rose violently again among the rest, but the subject had changed from politicos to noses.

José Fernandez was duly found, and acquitted at first sight.

Having inspected the drivers available in front of the Customs House, Del resumed tramping with the long wide way of the Embarcadero before him.

He went into dubious bars and waterside cafés whenever he saw an untended cab nearby. Night had come on and he was hungry and tired. He bought food and drink and sat a while, afflicted by the discouraging thought that the man he was looking for was no licensed driver but a hired thug in a peaked cap.

When he resumed the search, he had a feeling that he was being followed. He halted, ostensibly to light a cigarette, and a heavily built man behind him stopped to peer into a window. Then, after a few more tests, his suspicion became a certainty. Distance was varied, but always the man came along on his trail.

Del hesitated. The neighbourhood was not of the sort that he would have selected for a promenade. It might be quite respectable, but it certainly looked doubtful and could well be a stamping-ground of the local underworld.

He was heading for a dark and lonely stretch that led towards the fishermen's wharves. He did not doubt that he could master his shadow in a stand-up fight, but he was not going to invite disaster. The fellow might be armed.

Del hastened his steps and turned the corner into a side street. A few minutes later he turned another corner and found himself in a thoroughfare that ran parallel to the Embarcadero. It was a narrow way but reasonably lighted and fairly populous with the patrons of bars and other night haunts.

Still the shadow came on behind him, and by now he was convinced that the big fellow was a footpad, a cautious footpad, ready to wait until he could get his quarry in a favourable spot.

Irritation grew to anger in the quarry. The situation was putting him off his stride when his first need was to concentrate on his search. He looked for a means to shake the fellow off, and a minute later saw his chance.

Fifty yards ahead of him a taxi set down a fare in front of a neon sign that announced chop suey to the tropical night.

Del sprinted and hopped into the cab.

"Embarcadero!" he ordered the driver. "Customs House! Hurry!"

Any place, anywhere would do. There was no other cab in the street. The shadow was beaten.

The driver took two corners riskily, sped along the Embarcadero, and stopped.

"Customs House," he announced. "Closed for the night. Nobody home."

Del felt for his pesos as he stepped to the pavement. Then he saw the long nose and receding chin of his rescuer. He grabbed.

"What's the matter?" the driver demanded. "Hands off, and pay your fare."

"One moment! You're the man who was hired to meet Señorita Page this morning."

"Señorita Page?" The driver peered. "Si, si! The *Atacama*. You were with her, yes?"

"Yes." Del took a firmer grip on the man's arm.

"She expected to go to the Granada. She didn't arrive there. Where did you take her?"

"What's that to you? Where my fares go is their business. Give me my money and get off my cab."

Del flourished a fist under the long nose. "I'll give you this if you don't answer me. Where did you take the girl?"

The man flailed round with his free arm and caught Del on the side of the head, and instantly the threatening fist made contact with his receding chin.

"Police!" he yelled. "Police!"

"Go on!" Del shouted. "Keep yelling till someone comes. Then we'll drive to the nearest police station. That's what I want. Do you hear? That's what I want."

"You want?"

Leaning back as far as he could, the driver stared into the face of his frenzied assailant.

Del pulled him forward. "If you won't talk to me, you'll talk to Inspector Chavez."

"Chavez?"

"So you know the name? Start your engine and get going."

"No, no, señor. It is a mistake. I've done nothing wrong. I am an honest man."

"Police headquarters can decide how honest you are. Get going!"

"Please, señor!" Truculence had dissolved into pleading servility. "I have a wife and family. I swear by all the angels I have done no crime. I did not think there was anything wrong. Please, señor, if you will be calm, I will tell you about the señorita."

"Tell me!"

"I followed instructions, you understand. How was I to suspect anything? The one who hired me was a gentleman, a true aristocrat. We start from the pier to go to the Granada, and suddenly the young English lady is ill. The gentleman is very alarmed. 'Quick,' he says. 'Never mind the hotel. I will take her to my place. My neighbour is a doctor.' Then he gives me the address and makes me turn."

"How could she have become ill?" Del closed his eyes tightly to check an attack of something that was like vertigo. "When she left the ship, she was as well as I am."

"Nevertheless, señor, I assure you. She was in a dead faint. I had to help the gentleman to carry her to his house."

"That's enough. We're going to the police. You can tell me the rest on the way."

"No. They will take away my licence. My family will starve."

"I'll see that you don't lose your licence. Now drive!"

"No, no, no! They have accused me once before when I was innocent. They will not believe me."

He was obviously too fearful to be moved in the direction of headquarters except by force. Del, in his impatience, accepted the possible alternative.

"All right," he agreed. "Tell me where you took your passengers."

"The house is in the Hermosa district, by Amarillo Creek."

"Drive me there, and be quick about it!"

The route lay along the Embarcadero and went on past the wharves of the fishing-boats. Then the road curved away from the sea on a wide arc and traversed a desolate stretch of low scrub. It looked like a mangrove swamp, but in the dim light Del could not be sure.

"Is it far to the place?" he demanded.

"Not far now." The man was frightened and his voice made it plain. Distant lights were visible through a screen of timber.

"Drive faster," Del ordered. "There is no traffic."

"I am doing my best. The engine is not so good."

At last they were in a street of fairly substantial houses with gaps that might once have been gardens between. The neighbourhood was shabby, conveying an air of neglect. Few of the windows showed lights.

"It is the last house but four on the right," the driver announced. "The Villa Miranda."

"Slow down and I'll hop off," Del instructed him. "You can pull up at the end of the row and wait for me. I'll take a look. Then I'll go to the police."

He regretted the yielding that had brought him here without the police, but it had seemed at the time the only way to deal with the driver. He had mistrusted the man, fearing that he might be fobbed off with a false address. Even now he suspected trickery.

There was not a soul in the road to observe him as he alighted, but he stood motionless for a moment in the darkness between two widely-spaced street lamps.

He watched the receding rear lights of the cab. Then he cursed. His mistrust was justified all too soon. Instead of pulling up at the end of the row of houses, the driver went on at increasing speed and the cab disappeared round a bend in the road. The noise of the engine died in the distance and silence was broken only by a slow rhythmic murmur of waves on a nearby beach.

Del blamed himself bitterly for not having forced the man to take him to Chavez. He had noted the number of the cab, but this was of no use to him now that he was stranded in this dismal neighbourhood. If the driver had not lied, Anne might still be in that shadowy house across the road, and, unless he acted on his own initiative, there must inevitably be a considerable delay before anything could be done about it.

It was the darkest hour of his day for him as he moved towards the Villa Miranda, but he was not the only one in a bitter mood at that moment. Back at headquarters, Chavez, too, was cursing, but not in self-blame. An underling had to take the stream of the inspector's invective, and the stream came to an end only when the switchboard operator connected the fuming officer with his first assistant.

"Send out an urgent alert!" Chavez shouted into the phone. "Traffic, patrols, all squad cars. I want the driver of hackney licence AY two-three-eight. Bring him in at once. Repeat: AY two-three-eight. At once, at once, at once!"

CHAPTER XXI

THE HOUSE appeared to be deserted. A vague mass in the night, it stood about four yards back from the road in what had once been a cultivated garden but was now a wilderness of weeds and overgrown shrubs.

Del opened a broken picket gate and went cautiously up a tiled path to the front door. He listened intently for a sound from within, but heard only that gentle sough of waves from the nearby beach. No hint of light showed between the slats of Venetian blinds behind the windows.

He moved carefully along a path to the rear and returned along the other side. Everywhere there was darkness and silence, and the adjacent houses seemed as deserted as this one, and just as dilapidated. But for a glimmer or two from windows some distance down the road, the whole neighbourhood appeared to be dead.

Once more he cursed the long-nosed driver, yet he could not be sure that he had been duped. Chavez might listen to him and search the house, but Chavez was a long way from the spot.

He was moving to take another look at the back premises when a faint sound made him doubly alert. A thin slit of light broke the darkness; a dim ray, as instantaneous as the quick flick of a camera's shutter.

It might have been caused by the movement of a blind or the opening of a door, but it was not from the house. It came from some distance in the rear.

Again he went cautiously along the side path. A tangled back garden of fruit trees and lush grass sloped gently downward, and the path, overgrown in places, led him on.

Now the shape of a tall out-building loomed against the lower stars; a strange structure, resembling a barn more than anything else. Like the house, it was dark and seemingly deserted, yet Del was sure it was the source of that momentary gleam.

Listening intently, he heard a lapping of water, and when he moved closer he realised that it came from within. Puzzled, he passed stealthily to the far end and there found the explanation.

The structure was a clapboard boat-house on a tidal creek or inlet, and the upper floor, probably a sail-loft, roofed a dock or landing-stage. The tide was coming in through an open gateway, lapping at the timbers. At the full, it would furnish enough water for a small craft to enter or leave. And from above a dim lamp shone through a dingy window, as if it had been put there to guide someone in from the creek; someone who might arrive at any moment.

Panic held Del rigid for a moment. Anne was here, and in imminent danger of being taken away. The obvious conclusion was that the kidnapper had held her here all day, waiting for nightfall and high tide. With the tide rising rapidly, there was no time to waste. Before he could bring the police, it would be too late.

The light through the dingy window revealed the rail of a narrow balcony that appeared to run round the whole of the upper floor. No doubt there were steps to this gallery somewhere on the garden side, but Del did not look for them. Retreating a little from the creek, he measured the height, leaped, got a hold on the flooring, and raised himself till he could reach the lower railing.

It was an easy matter to gain the balcony after that, and he made a quick examination. There were windows along the side, but they were all obscured by dark blinds. He could see no means of entry, so he moved with cat-quiet steps till he was crouching below the lighted pane at the seaward end. Then he rose up slowly and looked inside.

The loft was a storehouse of marine junk and other rubbish: old sails, broken timbers, lengths of rope, discarded paint pots, fishing tackle, petrol cans. At the far end, his back to the window, a man lolled on a packing-case, reading a paper. Del rubbed some of the grime from the pane, raised himself another inch, and looked again.

Anne was lying on a canvas camp-bed, apparently asleep.

Del took in the essential details carefully. There was a door at the far end, and it must have been the momentary opening of this that he had seen from the garden. Since it had been used so recently, the chances were that it would yield to a push. There were no bolts on it; only a heavy, old-fashioned lock. Del peered, but could not decide whether there was a key in the lock; the light supplied by a single hurricane-lamp was too dim.

The solitary guard was a big fellow, obviously an awkward customer. If he were alert, he must see any movement of the door, but it would take him a moment to get on to his feet and another split second might be gained by surprise. From the door to his packing-case was about three yards; a quick step and a leap as Del measured it.

In the silence the lapping of water was loud. If a craft was coming, it must come very soon.

Del went quietly but swiftly along the side gallery towards the door, going over his plan of attack as he did so.

It worked out perfectly up to a point. The door was unlocked. Del crashed it open and made his leap. The guard, giving a shout, dropped his newspaper and sprang up just in time to be toppled over the packing-case. But he was too tough to be put out by one blow. He came back with a knife in his hand.

Del grappled. Weight was against him, but he was strong, and a trick he knew served him well. The knife fell to the floor, to be kicked aside. Del broke away and poised himself for another assault.

A hard jolt to the jaw made the enemy grunt. Del followed it up, missed with a left, and was sent back by a painful blow on the side of the head. Then muscular arms were round him in a crushing hug. He went down, bringing the man with him, and they rolled on the boards, clutching and striking at one another.

Del was first on his feet, and as his opponent came at him with fists swinging wildly, he dodged easily and found his mark with a counter of shaking force. Then he went in, knowing just what he had to do. There was no law of fair play in this sort of brawl. He crashed home a right well below the belt and followed it with an uppercut to a wide-open jaw.

The man went down, his head thudding on the floor. He was half stunned, rolling in agony, with Del on top of him, pounding him till he blacked out.

Anne had not moved. The panting Del ran to the camp-bed and shook her.

"Anne!" he called. "Anne!"

A noise from the doorway made him turn, and shock caused him to step back involuntarily. He was looking into the barrel of a revolver, and behind the weapon he saw a long thin face with a greying goatee at the end of it.

"Put up your hands!"

A gesture with the pistol supplemented the calmly spoken order.

It was stupefying, dazing. The bitterness of defeat and his frantic anxiety for Anne produced a feeling of nausea. He heard the order repeated. He heard the chug-chug of an engine from the creek outside, and slowly he raised his hands.

"Keep them up!"

The intervener was tall and lean and well groomed and completely at ease. Keeping his pistol levelled, he reached behind him with his free hand and turned the key that Del had failed to see. Then he moved to the rail-guarded opening of a stairway that gave access to the dock below.

He waited. The engine outside gave a few more chugs and a splutter and a beam of white light played up through the stair hatch, a beam that moved to the undulations of the water and grew in brightness as the craft in the creek came nearer.

Del watched, fully alert again, determined to risk an attack if the man relaxed. He was on his toes, ready to spring. There would be a moment, surely, when the movement below must distract the fellow.

The engine cut out and the launch glided into the boathouse with a faint rasping of timbers against the dock. But the man with the pistol did not relax. With his eyes on Del and his trigger-finger ready, he called down the stairway.

"Dino!" he called. "Come up here at once. Bring Felipe with you."

Dino was an under-sized, worn-looking Italian in grease-smudged overalls. He stared at Del with alarm in his eyes.

"What is this?" he demanded. "Who is the fellow?"

"A friend of the girl's. I saw him at the pier. She told me he was going on to Antofagasta. It is unfortunate for him that he changed his plan."

"But how did he come here?"

"Ask him. Possibly he ran across my cab-driver."

Dino swore. "I told you how it would be, Balaguer. It was madness to pick up a taxi on the Embarcadero."

"What could I do?" Balaguer pointed to the stunned man on the floor. "That clown failed to turn up with the car. Could I show myself on the ship?" He shrugged. "You have no need to worry, my friend. You will have another passenger for a while. That is all. The girl will give you no trouble. She will sleep for an hour yet, and when she wakes —"

Del broke in on him wildly. "What are you going to do to her?"

Balaguer smiled. "You are in no position to ask questions, señor," he said. "She will, perhaps, be in good hands. The one you have to worry about is yourself."

"If anything happens to her, you'll answer for it."

"To whom, señor? To you?" Balaguer wheeled. The revolver was lowered, but the odds were too much for Del. There were three of them, all barring the way to the door, and Dino's man was a burly ox of a fellow.

"Tie him up, Felipe," Balaguer ordered.

"What am I to do with him?" Dino demanded.

"That is entirely for your discretion." Balaguer pocketed his revolver. "There is no need for me to suggest the details."

Del struggled as Felipe came at him with a length of rope, but his resistance was quickly overcome. Then, as he was helpless, his hands tied behind him, Dino went through his pockets and his wallet was transferred to the smeared overalls.

"A souvenir!" Dino exclaimed. "A nice fat souvenir. Enough to pay for many masses."

The stunned man came to life, groaning and shifting and feeling his bruises. Balaguer prodded him with a foot.

"Get up, you!" he ordered. "There's work to do. Give Felipe a hand to get the cases on board." He turned to Dino. "You have no time to spare if you're going to use the tide."

The two men started down the stairs, but Dino lingered.

"Have you heard anything from up-river?" he asked. "I'm worried about that shooting business."

"Newspaper talk!" Balaguer was impatient. "The trucks will be waiting at the usual point below Guadelemo. Now get the girl on board, and see that there is no accident. You are to deliver her unharmed. I'll make your other passenger ready for you."

"You can leave him to me. You and Larreta are too fond of that damned needle."

Dino lifted the sleeping Anne and started towards the stairway with her. Del pulled and wrenched to get his hands free, moved by an impulse beyond reason. He was helpless. He had only his voice to use, and he used it in his frenzy. He shouted for help with all the power that he had.

Balaguer answered the anxious look of Dino with a grimace. "He might yell for ever," he said. "There is no one to hear."

Dino went on down the stairs with his burden.

Del gave another shout, but it was merely the voice of his frustration. He heard the lapping of water. He heard the slithering and thudding of heavy cases being moved to Dino's craft. And he contrived a last slender hope out of his desperation.

He could not free his hands, but he had the use of his legs and only one man to deal with.

Balaguer, his back turned, was doing something at a cupboard near the door.

A sudden charge would send him sprawling, a kick might disable him, and before help could reach him from below, Del would be out in the night and running for the first tenanted house. He would demand aid. He would telephone to Chavez. The launch would be

141

overtaken before it could get very far.

Del took a cautious step towards the cupboard. He glanced at the door, but the difficulty of opening it did not deter him. Somehow he would manage to turn the key.

He moved another step. He gauged the distance carefully, but in the last split second of preparation for the charge, Dino came hurrying up the stairs.

"Most of the stuff is on board," he announced. "We'll be ready in one minute."

Balaguer turned from the cupboard with a hypodermic syringe in his hand. He nodded, and Dino knew what to do. Del was gripped from behind. His jacket was hauled back and down from his shoulders. His shirt was wrenched open and torn and an arm was partly bared for the needle.

Del doubled and plunged and kicked out. Dino shifted his grip and threw him and held him down. The needle pricked the bared flesh and went in.

"So," Balaguer said. "He'll be calm in a moment."

Del was pulled to his feet and pushed towards the stairway. He was panting, his pulse hammered. More slithering and thudding sounds reached him. Then there was a different kind of thudding, like the noise of running feet, and a shrill, imperative whistle was blown in the garden.

Dino let go of him and dashed down the stairs, calling to Balaguer to follow him. Now the thudding was on the door of the loft and the whistle sounded again and again.

Del broke away as Balaguer tried to force him towards the stairway. He saw then that the man was left with only a frantic urge to escape, and he barred the way to the stairs. If he could cause a delay, if Dino waited for Balaguer, they might all be taken and Anne would be safe.

Balaguer came at him, swinging a fist. Del side-stepped and kicked. He kicked savagely, and the lean man fell back with a cry of pain, his right hand reaching for the revolver in his pocket. The door splintered and shook under heavy blows, yet it held. Dino was still yelling urgent advice to Balaguer, but suddenly his voice was cut off by the roar of his craft's engine.

Vibrations that seemed to start a trembling in the whole fabric of the boathouse had a shattering effect on Del. He felt sick. His legs were weak and aching and he caught at the rail of the hatch for support. A heavy drowsiness threatened him and it was difficult for him to keep his eyes open. Fumes of burnt oil were rising above him and he turned to get away from the stairway.

He saw the levelled revolver through a haze and he started on a stumbling run at Balaguer. The sound of a shot snapped through the engine noise, and he rocked back, lost his balance, and fell.

For a moment he lay as if all power to move had gone from him, but somehow he found a little strength to raise himself on his hands and knees. The splintered door gave way at last, and he saw Chavez as the police rushed through the opening.

He tried to get to his feet, but collapsed on the floor. A dark wave was rising to draw him away, right away, and Chavez could not save him. To get a word out was an enormous strain.

"The river," he said. "They're making for the river."

He wanted to tell Chavez about Anne, but the wave rose over him and he was gone.

CHAPTER XXII

WHEN HE woke up his head was throbbing and his left shoulder seemed to have solidified into a piece of masonry. But, like his head, the masonry was aching. He was lying, not quite straight out but nearly so, on what seemed to be a cushioned lounge-seat, something like a dentist's chair that had been racked back to an almost horizontal position. When he moved he felt a sharp pain in his shoulder, and this caused him to relax at once. Then he realised that he was staring up at an absurdly low ceiling, and the room seemed to be swaying.

He studied the sensation for a while. There was no doubt about the oscillation. He had just cleared that up when the whole room made a sudden swooping descent, like a lift plunging down an incline. After it had levelled out, he ignored the painful shoulder and tried to raise himself in the dentist's chair.

Chavez said: "So you are awake at last! That is good, but please take it easy, señor."

"Where are we?" Del asked.

"We are in a plane on the way to Trajano. The coastal range is below us and there have been some bad patches."

"What's the matter with my shoulder?"

"You were hit by a bullet, but it is nothing much. You will have an inconvenience for a few days."

Del was trying to grasp everything at once. "Anne?" he cried suddenly. "Did you stop them? Is she safe?"

For the first time Chavez knew for a fact what he had suspected: the missing Anne Page was on the launch that had got away.

He spoke hopefully, out of concern for the young man, but the girl was an insignificant item in his thoughts. He was exultant. He saw promotion at last, an elevation to glory.

"This is a time for prompt action," his chief had told him, with generous enthusiasm. "Fly to Trajano with your witness, and at last you will be able to convince the doubters. The Commissioner's own plane is here, waiting to go back. I will arrange it."

"Will there be no objection?" Chavez asked nervously, remembering the notoriety of the Commissioner as a difficult type.

"When the salvation of the country is in the balance, objections must be overruled."

It was a nice phrase, even if the chief had caught some of his subordinate's nervousness in it. The Commissioner's pilot had certainly raised no objection to jumping his schedule. He was only too anxious to get back to Trajano. And the last of the inspector's doubts had died in the fire of a rosy dawn over the Andes.

Chavez, the saviour of his country, urged his fellow passenger to cast out dismay.

"The whole police force of San Mateo will go into action," he said. "If necessary, the army will be mobilised."

"The army? To find the launch?" Del asked, pressing his hands to his bumping head.

"To stamp out the insurrection. Bartol will never be allowed to set foot again on the soil of our country."

"Who the hell is Bartol?" Del demanded. "Don't you realise that Anne Page is on that launch? Why are you taking me to Trajano?"

"To see the Police Commissioner himself. The chief of my department is arranging an appointment by telephone. Perhaps at this very moment he is on the line, talking to the great man."

He was, but the great man was doing most of the talking.

"You get me out of bed at daybreak for this?" he roared. "You have the temerity to commandeer my plane – my own plane – for this?"

"But the plane was going to leave in a few hours. The pilot said he was free, once he had seen the Peruvian general on his way to Lima."

"I will sack the pilot. I will sack you. I will sack that imbecile Chavez. A cheap smuggler runs off in a broken-down launch, and you conclude that Bartol is ready to march on the Capital."

"But, Excellency, the launch is making its way up the Medina River. I don't think you realise –"

"*Madre de Dios,* I realise that I have been dragged from my sleep! Enough, enough!"

The Commissioner slammed the receiver down and turned over in bed. The result of it all was that he overslept and he reached his office late and in one of his worst moods. After he had kept Chavez and Del waiting for an hour, he saw them. He was freezingly polite for a few minutes. Then the lava broke through the ice and in another moment he was in full eruption.

"One case of pop-guns in an abandoned boat-house!" he thundered.

"Pardon, Excellency," Chavez answered. "A case of the most modern machine-guns, left behind because of my timely raid. And Señor Wayne will tell you that many cases were loaded on to the launch. He heard them."

"He heard them, but did he see them? For all he knows, the cases may have been full of butter or toy trains."

For once Chavez lost his head.

"Desperate men do not smuggle butter or toy trains," he snapped back. "I bring you proof that guns are being run into the country. What more do you want? For all any of us know, this launch may have made a dozen trips up the river in the last two months."

"You are in charge of the waterfront at Santa Teresa, and this is all you know! Señor Wayne overhears talk of a river, and from this you create an army in hiding. Where are these guns being landed up the river? Tell me that."

"A place was mentioned, but unfortunately Señor Wayne cannot recall it. You must remember that he has just come through a very bad experience. He is still not over the effects."

"That is a pity. Señor Wayne should be more careful of the company he keeps. He gets in a brawl over a girl because she goes off with these men, and you have to build an insurrectionary mare's nest out of it."

Hot blood was pounding in Señor Wayne's suffering head. "Listen to me!" he exploded. "I don't give a damn for your insurrections and your mare's nests. Anne Page has been kidnapped by a bunch of gangsters. What are you going to do about it? I want to know, and I want to know at once, before you waste any more valuable time."

"That's enough!" The Commissioner rose, red-faced in wrath. "You will learn, young man, that you cannot dictate to me. Any action that may be necessary will be taken. You, Chavez, are to return to Santa Teresa at your own expense. Your future in the service will be considered by my committee. Meanwhile you are suspended from duty."

"The fat pig!" Chavez exclaimed when they were out in the street. "I have always suspected that he is a Bartolista. Now I know." Then, as cold dismay put out his heat, he was a small man, beaten and afraid. "What shall I do?" he moaned. "My wife, my children! What shall I do?"

"Lend me some money," Del answered, and hailed a passing taxi. "The Opera!" he shouted to the driver as he pushed Chavez into the cab.

"But it is just across the Plaza," the surprised Chavez protested.

"Quickly!" Del called to the driver. "Stage door!"

The uniformed janitor was formidable and unsympathetic. He was prepared to concede that Don Sebastian Byrne was within, but no callers were permitted to enter without the authority of the director. Rehearsal was about to begin.

Del nudged Chavez, and the inspector produced his badge.

"My dear Del!" Don Sebastian behaved as if they were bosom friends reunited after years of separation. "How is it you are not on the way to Chile?"

Del explained how it was. The more he explained, the more excited Sebastian became.

"Anne!" he cried. "It is impossible, incredible! She must be saved. At once."

"That's why I've come to you. As Minister of Fine Arts, your father may have some influence to move the police."

"Move them. He controls them. He is also Minister of the Interior.

He will act. This gun-running is a bad business. Carmen was right after all. Perhaps those shots along the river in the Guadelemo district were really —"

Sebastian was about to say significant, but Del broke in on him excitedly. "That's it! That's the place. The trucks are to be waiting below Guadelemo."

"It begins to make sense." Sebastian took his jacket from a hook. "Guadelemo is a mud village in the high hills above Rosario. You say that Julian Page is dead and Anne's father is missing. And it was Julian Page who found the uncut emerald at Rosario."

"What has that to do with it?"

"Perhaps everything. If the Bartolistas are at Guadelemo, they may be at Rosario as well. That Police Commissioner is an idiot."

"He is a Bartolista." A woeful Chavez spoke for the first time. "There is no other explanation."

Don Sebastian wheeled in the act of straightening his jacket. "Who are you?" he demanded.

Del interposed. "This is Inspector Chavez. It was he who pulled in that taxi-driver. If he hadn't acted so promptly, I wouldn't be here. He saved my life."

"Perhaps he has saved all our lives. Come, Chavez! We go at once to my father."

There was bustle in the corridor outside the dressing-room, and a perspiring figure in shirt-sleeves came rushing after them.

"Sebastian!" he called. "Where are you going? You are wanted on the stage at once. It is the Puccini."

"Devil take the Puccini!" Sebastian strode on. "I have something more important to do. Tell Bernardo he can rehearse *Lucia.*"

CHAPTER XXIII

PEPE PLEADED hoarsely for a drink, and there was no more water in the earthenware jug. Lewis hammered on the door of the adobe hut till the guard came.

"What do you do with all the water?" the man complained. "One would think I had nothing to do but fetch and carry for you. Give me the jug."

"When will the doctor be here?" Lewis demanded.

"How should I know? If you still feel bad, take another quinine pill."

"I am all right. It is Pepe. His wound needs attention."

"I will send up to the plateau for one of the ambulance men." The fellow had a gruff manner, but was not unkindly. When he brought the water, he poured some into a mug and raised Pepe so that he could drink.

"Is there anything you want for yourself?" he asked Lewis.

"A shave." Lewis rubbed the irritating stubble on his face. "If I could have a shave . . ."

"What do you think this is? The Grand Hotel? The orders are, no razors. The General would be offended if you cut yourself. Why do you object to a beard? A few more days, and you will look quite distinguished."

"A few more days! How long are we to be kept in this pigsty?"

"Till the revolution." The guard grinned.

"How long will that be?"

"It depends. Opportunity does not ripen in the sun. It takes money and organisation. We are only the advance party, the bridgehead. If you ask me, it will be a long time before everything is ready. Settle down, my friend. Be content with your beard. If it were not for the General's sister, you wouldn't be here to talk of razors."

"Where is she? What has become of her?"

"Naturally she is at the finca. I saw her yesterday when I went down to take a turn with a shovel." He laughed. "She is sad, if it is any consolation to you. Perhaps she is pining for you. Next time you should plan the elopement better."

It was no use protesting against the fellow's words. Lewis had learned that the "elopement" was the joke of the camp.

"She is a prisoner?" he asked. "Is that it?"

"We are all prisoners." The guard shrugged. "When Bartol returns, then will be the great liberation. I hope you will live that long."

"If I do, I will reward you for your kindness."

"Is this another attempt to bribe me?"

"It is not. Have you heard anything of my daughter?"

"I know nothing at all of your daughter."

"You promised to ask."

"I have asked. I know nothing. If she landed only yesterday, it is too early for news." He hesitated. "I have heard that a launch is coming up the river from the port. It should reach our landing some time to-morrow. That is all I can tell you, and now I must lock you up. When the ambulance man comes, you may go back to the plateau with him and take your walk."

With the hot sun pouring down on the mud walls, the hut was like an oven. Pepe slept in his corner till midday, when the guard brought soup and bread. It was good soup and wholesome bread, but Pepe would not eat. Lewis became more and more anxious about him.

The man from the ambulance unit did not come till after three. He was a cheerful fellow, singing as he came. They were mostly cheerful fellows, these liberators. In moments of relaxation they laughed and sang as if there were nothing serious in life. When they trained – and they had hours of training each day – they were grim fanatics, devoted to their cause.

"You will live if you don't get in the way of any more bullets," the ambulance man told Pepe.

He was expert. His hands had tenderness.

Lewis walked back with him to the plateau. Once a day he was to be allowed an hour or two of liberty in the open. He was free to move as he wished when his escort had brought him to the high place, because from there it was impossible to escape.

The plateau was a natural stronghold, approached through a narrow defile where machine-guns poked their muzzles through screening foliage.

Lewis looked back at the village from the entrance to the defile. Once the Indian families who still lived in the huts had earned money by picking coffee for Julian; now they were prisoners and servants of the rebels.

There were, perhaps, two hundred of these rebels, and some of them had made temporary homes in caves while others lived in much-used tents. They were boastful, like assertive children. The amiable ambulance man was particularly boastful.

Lewis probed him. "How do you think you can throw out the government with this handful?"

The young man laughed. "There are many more of us back in the hills, and once we move, the army will revolt. In all the towns our fifth column is ready. The people will rise in the streets. The first bullet will pierce the heart of the tyrant Recalde."

"Why do you wait, then?"

"General Izarbarra will not give the word until we have planes and pilots. He is a great organiser, our Pascual. Planes and pilots cost money, but we are digging it out of the earth down there. In green stones. Did you know that? Emeralds."

Emeralds!

Lewis remembered the green stones in the drawer of the desk at the Casa Alta. He remembered the ring that Julian had given to Anne.

The plateau was a wide terrace, looking out to the south over the jungle slope that bordered the Casa Alta; a great natural parade-ground, hidden and secured by a rough semi-circle of precipitous rock.

At this time of day it was deserted. All the rebels, except the sentries, were resting, waiting for the cooler hours.

Lewis crossed to the far edge of the terrace where a craggy projection afforded a view over a vast stretch of country through which the river wound. He strained to see to the utmost range of vision, but could find no craft on the river. If a launch was due at the landing tomorrow, it was still many miles away beyond the screening hills.

He walked slowly back along the edge of the jungle and paused for a moment at the beginning of a narrow track that vanished into the thick mass of greenery that ran down to the coffee terraces. No one used the track because it was too difficult, but a sentry was there to turn back a prisoner who might be tempted to try it.

"Buenas dias, señor."

The sentry grinned and brought up his rifle in a mocking gesture of salute. Like the rest of them, he wore a dull greenish battledress of tough gaberdine.

Lewis walked on a few yards. When he came back to the defile, his promenade would be over, and he had no wish to return to the hut just yet. He paused again.

Looking down over the tree-tops, he could see the roof of the Casa Alta and the gods and warriors in the forecourt. He watched, hoping that Leite might come from the house and cross the open space, but it seemed that no one was stirring.

He closed his eyes and the fear came to him that he would never see her again.

That was the moment when the first shot was fired.

It cracked loudly in the still clear air of the afternoon, and the sentry at the jungle path lifted his head as the echo rattled over the valley.

Three shots followed in quick succession and shouts could be faintly heard. Then a jumble of figures, small as ants, raced past the stone figures in the direction of the coffee terraces.

Men on the plateau sprang from their rest and ran. Some headed for the defile. Others came to the jungle edge and looked at one another questioningly.

There was nothing more for a long time. Then a submachine-gun chattered below them and Lewis knew that it was being fired from the track that climbed up the slope above the coffee trees.

He had joined the group of the alarmed men, but none of them took any notice of him. They were listening anxiously, seeking the answer to the riddle in their minds.

There was silence again, but not for long. A new burst of firing, more intense and prolonged, told them that the workers from the mine had joined battle. The men on the rim looked towards an officer who stood with them, but he was as puzzled as any of them and had no order to give.

Another officer ran towards them across the plateau. "It's the police," he shouted while he was still some yards away. "They have raided the house. That much came through. Then the field line went dead."

"So there has been a traitor!"

"What are we to do?"

"Orders are definite," the newcomer said. "Whatever happens at the house, we are not to reveal ourselves. If it is only the police, then they can have little information. Someone has become curious about the man Page. One of his friends, perhaps."

"But the General may be in danger!"

"It was he who gave us our orders. The house must at all times be disregarded. There is nothing to do but wait."

The heavy burst of firing had ended. Now there were only occasional shots, suggesting a pursuit through the jungle, but the intervals between them grew longer and longer and soon there was silence.

Hope rose higher and higher in Lewis. The day of the monster was over. Leite would be delivered from him, and Leite would see that Anne was safe.

He wiped the sweat from his face. The next moment he was cold under the hot sun. He shivered, but the ague was not physical. One of the officers became aware of him.

"Take that prisoner back to his hut," he ordered.

Lewis stumbled as he turned. Despair was in him again and his dejection was the deeper for the bright hope that had gone. The raid on the finca may have upset Pascual's plans, but it could not have been decisive. Pascual was not a man to be caught so easily, and it would take more than a detachment of rural police to overcome Guadelemo.

The guns in the defile were manned, and beyond the village the outposts waited.

CHAPTER XXIV

PASCUAL EMERGED from the jungle and climbed over the rim of the plateau with ten of his men trailing behind him. In appearance he was a wreck, his face scratched and swollen, his torn shirt marked by a wide spread of clotted blood; but the spirit in him was steel hard.

He gave no explanation. He had time only for orders. When an anxious lieutenant expressed concern, he silenced him.

"Send Morales to me," he snapped. "The signal goes out at once. All operations will commence at four in the morning."

The lieutenant's heart gave a bump. The programme of careful preparation had weeks to run. Now everything was to be risked in a sudden gamble. The lieutenant wanted to expostulate, but saw that it was no use. The case had become one of expediency.

An hour later, at six o'clock, Dr. Larreta drove his car through the defile and made his way to the cave where Pascual waited for him.

Larreta's nerves had become such a knot of terror that he screamed at the man he had always feared.

"I warned you," he screamed. "I told you it was dangerous to let the girl come on from England. As soon as I heard about that telephone call from Santa Teresa yesterday, I knew there would be trouble with the police. The girl is responsible for this mess."

"The girl walked off the ship straight into the trap," Pascual answered him. "She spoke to no one but Balaguer."

"Balaguer always was a bungler. Now we will be shot down like rats. All of us. Like rats."

"Stop being hysterical. You will live to be hanged. Now attend to me. I have lost much blood. I am tired. I must get my strength back."

Larreta worked with shaking hands. "Mother of God, what a state you are in! Where is Manuel? He could have done something for you."

"Manuel is dead."

Larreta straightened himself and stared. "And Leite? She is in the hands of the police, I suppose."

Pascual shook his head. "I sent her away yesterday, to Maria Josefa. She was of no further use; more of a hindrance. Leite was the one mistake. She is a fool. She has a conscience. We could have picked up a woman in Trajano and done better."

"You sent her to Maria Josefa! Now I understand."

"What do you understand?"

"It is Leite who has betrayed us, and it is not to be wondered at after the way you treated her."

"Imbecile! Get on with your work. Leite would die before she would speak a word."

"You do not understand women. You bring her here to be the wife of a dead man and she falls in love with the living brother. Isn't that enough for you, or are you blind to everything in your egomania?"

"There is one thing you are blind to, my friend. In one week, in less than a week, I shall control San Mateo. It is just as well that we are forced to quick action. We may lose a little more blood, but less money. And Bartol will be left to go on dithering in his exile. We will require his name no longer."

"Bartol is fortunate. He has something to be thankful for."

"And you! You will have something to be thankful for when you are my Minister of Health. Now patch me up and give me some benzedrine."

"You must get some sleep. You are exhausted."

"Give me some benzedrine. I can't afford to sleep. Not to-night."

Larreta sat down on the end of the cot and covered his face with his hands. Pascual jerked himself up, wincing.

"What is the matter with you now?" he demanded. "Are you weeping?"

"Before I left my house," the doctor answered slowly, "I spoke to my son in Trajano. There are rumours that troops are on the way."

"Good!" Satisfaction leaped in the voice. "That's what I want. We will eat up those cringing loyalists of Trajano. It will be well to have them out of the way, for the rest of the army is mine. To-morrow Guadelemo will be a new name in the military history of our Republic."

To-morrow . . .

Stimulated by the tablets that Larreta had given him, Pascual worked strenuously and waited impatiently for the signal hour.

But the cringing loyalists did not wait. They attacked at three in the morning.

The rebel outposts were driven in without difficulty. Some of them panicked, and the panic spread to the machine-gunners, who disclosed their positions by firing at shadows. At dawn the six bombers of the San Mateo Air Force came over and blew a lot of rock out of the sides of the defile.

While the bombers were on their way back to reload, General San Martin de la Cerda launched his first assault, but was checked by machine-gun fire. At six o'clock the Trajano Broadcasting Service interrupted its physical jerks programme to announce that Guadelemo had fallen to the Government troops and that the rebels were bottled up in a hopeless position.

At six-ten a nervous sergeant on a round-up of snipers kicked open the door of a mud hut, pushed his rifle inside, and yelled "Hands up!"

Lewis willingly raised his hands and expressed himself gratefully in hasty Spanish. The sergeant was suspicious, but before he had time to ask a question, a bullet whanged into the doorway, just missing him, and he threw himself down, tumbling Lewis to the floor in the process.

The moment was recorded as six hours thirteen minutes in the official communique. General Izarbarra had sprung his trap and the second phase of the battle of Guadelemo had begun.

A battalion of men in war-surplus battledress had come down from the higher hills to pour a withering fire on the loyalists, but in a very short time the government troops were under cover and there was nothing to wither.

Recovered from the surprise, General de la Cerda exercised

extreme caution, and the second phase developed as drearily and almost as painlessly as an exercise on autumn manoeuvres. After the first battery of the Trajano Mobile Artillery had shelled the hills, the air force came over with intent to bomb the same positions, but most of their load fell on or near the village.

The village, indeed, took the brunt of the whole action, and it was anything but brunt-proof. The adobe houses, deserted except for the one occupied by Lewis and Pepe and the nervous sergeant, collapsed in heaps of rubble or went up in dust. Bullets whizzed from all directions to thud into mud walls or splinter the doors.

At ten o'clock, Trajano radio announced that a town in the north-east, near the Colombian border, had fallen to the insurgents. As if heartened by the news, Pascual's men made a sortie from the defile in armoured trucks, but were forced back after losing two of the vehicles.

Reports of risings here and there throughout the country were given out by the radio in the next hour, always with the addition that the government troops claimed to have the situation well in hand. Rebellious cadets had been isolated in their own barracks, a rising in the working-class suburb of Santa Teresa had been put down, and at eleven o'clock it was reported that the lost town in the north-east had been recaptured by the government.

At noon a refreshed air force really devastated the defile above Guadelemo, and General de la Cerda ordered a grand assault. His guns kept the men in the hills inactive, and the assault succeeded. At last the smashed village had a respite. Lewis and the sergeant brought Pepe from the remains of the prison hut, and, long before the battle of Guadelemo was over, Pepe was on his way to hospital in Trajano, and Lewis, instructed to see Inspector Chavez at police headquarters, travelled with him in the ambulance.

By three in the afternoon the only water-borne operation of the insurrection had been carried out. A motor launch, chugging up the river towards the landing below Guadelemo, surrendered to a police boat and a Customs cutter without firing a shot, and Anne, emerging from the cabin, was held tightly in Del's arms, watched by an embarrassed and slightly rueful Sebastian.

When the cutter landed them in Trajano, a waiting messenger informed them that Señor Lewis Page was at the Hotel Europa. Sebastian wished to disappear quietly. His work was done. He could go back to the Opera and die a deceived hero's death in the last act of "Tosca." But Anne and Del would not relinquish him to Sardou's firing-squad and he finally consented to go with them to the hotel.

CHAPTER XXV

THEY WERE a quiet party at dinner that night. They were even quieter when they took their coffee in the lounge and waited for news of the insurrection. Lewis was happy in the safety of Anne, but, with one anxiety resolved, he was the more worried over Leite.

Also, the cloud of Julian's death was oppressing him, and Anne, too, was saddened by it, though for her Julian had been a more or less legendary figure, and now she had a new interest to absorb her.

Lewis was glad of this. Delbert Wayne impressed him as an admirable, level-headed young man, and what his worldly position might be was of no consequence. Possibly, as an engineer, he drew a salary on which two might live in comfort, and a bankrupt father could ask for no more. The important thing was that Delbert Wayne had proved his devotion and shown his worth.

It was difficult to realise that a daughter could have become grown-up so suddenly and, in a moment, be so far removed. And worrying constantly about Leite, Lewis felt a loneliness that was aggravated rather than cured by these young people: the mercurial Don Sebastian, the confident and possessive Delbert Wayne, even the yielding Anne with her new courage and assurance. He was a fit companion only for this Inspector Chavez, who sat a little apart in a gloomy cloud of his own.

Chavez sipped his liqueur without interest. He was aware that he had performed a certain service to the Government, but he knew only too well the forgetfulness of the politicos, and at the end of this day he could contemplate only the facts. He was suspended, awaiting demotion. He would have to borrow the fare to get back to Santa

Teresa. Seven children to feed, and his wife near her time. . . .

Children and revolutions might come and go, but at the Europa the band played as gaily as ever in the ballroom, and the lights shone on fair women and – well, they could not all be brave men and go out and battle with the Bartolistas. One must have confidence in the army.

There had been no news since six o'clock, but no one on the dance floor seemed troubled. Only among the coffee drinkers in the lounge was there a lingering of anxiety.

Carmen entered with a party of friends and left them when she saw Sebastian.

"I told you how it would be, and you would not listen," she upbraided him. "Now we are trapped. All day I have been trying to get a seat on a plane. I needed your help, and you were nowhere to be found. What am I to do?"

"Calm yourself and go back to your friends," Sebastian advised her. "You excite yourself without reason."

"Without reason? How can you talk like that with half the country in the hands of the rebels?"

"I have not heard of it." Don Sebastian had risen to meet her, and he motioned now to his group. "If you wish to join us, I must introduce you to . . ."

She cut him off angrily. "You!" she condemned him. "Your father is in the Government and you have heard nothing! Perhaps you do not yet know that Bartol has landed by helicopter. By morning Trajano will be under gunfire."

"In that case you had better go to bed and get a good night's rest. There is a ballet call for ten in the morning."

"Ten! By ten the Opera House will be blown up and we will all be dead."

She turned her back on him. Her own friends were more sympathetic, no doubt, for it was obvious that they, too, were infected by fear.

Nervousness spread as rumours drifted in from the streets. People in the lounge gathered apprehensively in front of the radio set at the far end, but the broadcasting authority continued to transmit fight music. The regular news bulletin was timed for eleven, and the gathering audience waited impatiently. Gramophone record followed gramophone record, but at ten-thirty the needle was lifted from the disc then turning.

"This is Radio Trajano," an impassive voice said. "We are interrupting our programme for a special announcement."

Someone turned up the volume. All talk ceased and waiters stopped in their tracks. A moment of silence and the news came.

"The insurrection is over. A Government communique confirms earlier reports that the ill-planned coup of the Bartolistas has ended in a complete fiasco. General San Martin de la Cerda, commanding detachments from Trajano, has routed a rebel force near the village of Guadelemo, inflicting heavy casualties at negligible cost. Among those killed in action was the rebel leader, Pascual Izarbarra. Minor incidents are reported from different parts of the country, but the latest advices indicate that the Government is in full control everywhere."

Trajano cheered and went on dancing.

At midnight a message was broadcast from Enrique Bartol in exile. He had learned with profound regret that his name had been used in connection with certain disturbances reported from San Mateo. He wished to dissociate himself entirely from such disturbances.

"When I accepted the hospitality of a friendly neighbour," the ex-president went on, "I gave a solemn undertaking not to engage in any political activity, and those who know me need not be reminded that I am a man of my word. I have never had, nor have I now, any intention of returning to San Mateo."

"Maybe it is true," Don Sebastian commented. "Who is to say? It is a wolf who plays scapegoat, and the wolf is dead."

He was called to the telephone. When he returned, he spoke to Lewis.

"My father wishes to see you at his office early in the morning," he said. "Full reports of the raid on your brother's property have been examined, and there are, I understand, some very curious aspects. If you will permit me, Señor Page, I will call for you at nine o'clock."

CHAPTER XXVI

THE MORNING MANTLE of Dr. Byrne went definitely with the portfolio of the Interior. He was supported at his desk by a sharp-featured ascetic who was presented to Lewis as Señor Rivas, assistant to the Director of Public Prosecutions. The only suggestion of the dual role played by Dr. Byrne in the Government was the fine art with which he conducted the interview.

"We are much troubled about this conspiracy at Rosario, Mr. Page," he began. "It might help us if you can throw any light on the political opinions of your brother."

"So far as I know, he never had any," Lewis responded. "I am sure he took no part in the affairs of this country."

"That is your belief, but you cannot answer positively that he was not a supporter of the Bartolistas?"

"I can answer to my own satisfaction. Julian would never have taken any action against your Government. He regarded himself as a guest in this country."

"But at the time of Bartol's flight, he gave refuge to the criminal Izarbarra –"

"Under threat."

Dr. Byrne ignored the interruption. "And," he went on, "we find the same Izarbarra installed at the Casa Alta, claiming to act for his half-sister, the alleged widow of your brother."

"It could not have been Julian's fault that Izarbarra took advantage of the situation."

"Of what situation, Mr. Page? Of Don Julian's marriage to the notorious Leite Mayorga?"

"Notorious?" The questioning echo came from Lewis on a breath that was almost a gasp.

"You seem to resent the epithet, Mr. Page. Perhaps I should have said politically notorious. Had she attempted to enter this country under her own name, she would have been arrested immediately."

The words were an ice-cold clamp on Lewis.

"Is she under arrest?" he asked.

"She will be when we have traced her." Dr. Byrne leaned forward. "You seem very interested in her, Mr. Page. Sympathetically interested, to judge from your tone. Yet you must have seen her as an intervener between you and a considerable inheritance."

"My brother's money was his own affair."

"But you knew of the will he made during his last visit to England?"

"No."

"Indeed!" Dr. Byrne leafed through the papers in the file. "This is a copy of the document, yielded by bankers on the demand of our Señor Rivas." He nodded in the direction of the intent aide. "Our laws permit us to take very prompt action in a case of suspected murder."

"Then you, too, believe that my brother was murdered?"

"My suspicion is strong. I can say no more. You will see that this earlier will is concerned with bequests to you and your daughter. You are the residuary legatee insofar as you are to enjoy the income of the estate during your lifetime; then everything passes to your daughter. It is, of course, revoked if the later will is proved valid."

Dr. Byrne dived once more into the file and produced the later will.

"Do you identify your brother's signature on this document?"

"Yes. I saw it at the house. It is undoubtedly Julian's signature."

"You have no thought of challenging it?"

"How can I challenge it?"

Dr. Byrne smiled a little patronisingly. "Almost any lawyer might suggest grounds, Mr. Page. Mental incompetence, undue influence, threats and menaces. You were subjected to threats yourself. Do you not feel that you have been cheated?"

"Whatever I feel, I cannot contest any man's right to make

provision for his wife."

"If he has a wife."

"What do you mean?" Lewis jerked himself up in his chair.

"I have the certificate of marriage." Dr. Byrne motioned vaguely towards the file. "It appears to be as valid as the will, but our invaluable Rivas has established a curious flaw. On the day of the certificate's issue, Leite Mayorga was still an exile in the United States, and we allow no marriages by proxy in this country."

"She may have flown here for a day and returned to –"

Lewis halted in bewilderment.

"Returned to where?" Dr. Byrne inquired.

"She was a passenger on the plane that flew me from Cristobal."

Señor Rivas spoke at last. "We are trying to trace the magistrate who certified the marriage. He is reputed to be a Bartol sympathiser. He has disappeared."

"And there is no Señora Page to claim the legacy," Dr. Byrne added. "I think you may take it, Mr. Page, that your brother was never married to the Mayorga woman. The more I consider the case, the more I incline to the belief that he was involved with the Bartolistas only so far as he was made the victim of Izarbarra and his sister. Men may be induced to do strange things under the influence of drugs, so you may be right in accepting any signature as authentic. On the other hand, clever forgers have sometimes confused the most expert of handwriting specialists."

Lewis stared at him in silence while hope and fear shuttled in his mind. Hope was furtive and fear had many faces.

"Let me advise you, Mr. Page," Dr. Byrne said. "You will return to the Casa Alta and take your daughter with you. It is necessary that someone should be in charge of the household, and you are the logical person.

Señor Rivas will go with you. He will have control of the police and will continue his investigations."

He paused to scribble a name and a street number on a card. "Meanwhile, I suggest that you see this man. He is a friend of mine and thoroughly reliable. He will look after your legal interests and secure the release of funds for you as quickly as possible."

Señor Rivas had a whispered word for the ear of his chief. Dr. Byrne nodded and turned to Lewis.

"There is one other matter, Mr. Page. It is clear that Izarbarra's acts at the Casa Alta were motivated by the discovery of an abandoned emerald mine on the estate. I have to warn you that all mineral rights are the property of the Republic. In the usual course, a claim for compensation is considered as soon as an assessment has been made. I hope you will find things not too difficult at Rosario. If I can be of assistance, you will please let me know."

CHAPTER XXVII

THINGS WERE NOT too difficult. The police had seen to it that the servants had gone about their usual courses, and Rivas helped Lewis to get a new order running smoothly. But Lewis was more concerned about Leite than he was about the household.

Fear for her was a constant obsession; fear that she was alone and in distress, fear that she would be found and arrested, fear that he would never see her again. All he could learn from the servants was that she had quarrelled violently with Izarbarra after the jungle adventure and that she had been driven away in a car the next day.

It might be, then, that she had got away from San Mateo in time. She had many friends, no doubt. There was her aunt, Maria Josefa. . . .

Lewis consulted Rivas, but it had already been established that the notorious woman had not sought refuge with Señora Mayorga, or, if she had, had been turned away in quick time.

"Doña Maria Josefa is under house arrest, pending a full investigation," Rivas said. "She is a great and respected lady who has always refused to involve herself in politics, but in affairs of this sort we take no chances. The Mayorgas have been a very troublesome family in our history, and it is known that Maria Josefa has always had an affection for her niece."

"Where is it that she lives?"

"The Casa Arenales is in the next valley to the south."

"Then it is not many miles away?"

"Not many, but it is useless to think of going there. The police will not permit you to see her."

"Possibly you could arrange it?"

"No, señor. That is something beyond me. When the case is cleared, you may visit her. Personally, I have no suspicion of the lady. However fond she might be of her niece, she would never have approved of what happened here."

Lewis knew that this was true. He remembered her as a hard, arrogant old woman, but surely she would have given help to a contrite Leite in desperate trouble.

"I will make inquiries," Rivas volunteered. "As soon as there is news, I will inform you."

Day after day Lewis waited, but Rivas always shook his head.

There was much to do on the estate. Resisting servants who had been removed to Guadelemo as Izarbarra's prisoners now returned to the house, and among them was the plantation overseer. Work along the coffee terraces was resumed, and Lewis was required to give assent to many things he did not understand.

Experts from the Mines Department arrived, and with them came prying archaeologists, old friends of Julian's, with a new interest in Rosario. Anne and Del were absorbed in these activities, so far as absorption in one another permitted. Had he been able to rouse himself from his gloom, Lewis, too, might have been excited, for it was soon made clear that here, on the jungle-covered hillside, was one of the mines that the conquistadores had failed to find.

The experts laughed over the story. The Indians had buried their jaguar-toothed god in the adit to foil the invaders from Spain, and time had had to wait for the coming of the absurd Englishman to rescue the stone image from its utilitarian office and restore it to the dignity of a pedestal; the absurd Englishman who had casually picked up an emerald and not bothered to look for more.

What the hill would yet yield in the way of precious loot was, of course, a matter for conjecture. It might be another Muzo. It might be, as Don Sebastian put it, an *affaire flambée,* a flash in the prospector's pan. Certainly it would now provide no guns or planes for the Bartolistas.

Whenever he could tear himself away from being shot at dawn in the rehearsals of *Tosca* Sebastian rushed up to the Casa Alta to inspect the latest crop of green stones. But perhaps the emeralds were just an excuse he made for himself. Hope died hard in Don Sebastian.

Soon came another, a more ominous visitor, who dropped frowning from the skies, uttering savage threats and flourishing an invincible cheque-book, but it took little more than a smile from Anne to reduce his blood pressure.

Never had there been so instantaneous a change in such a wilful parent.

"What the devil are you waiting for?" Beckett Wayne inquired almost plaintively of his son. "You don't deserve anything like this, you great hobbledehoy. And you led me to believe she was a fortune-hunting adventuress!"

"You can't blame me for your evil mind. I described her as a perfect angel. What more do you want?"

"It's your misguided sense of economy. If you had paid for a few more words, I would have understood. For heaven's sake marry the girl before she changes her mind. And get along to Antofagasta. I'll send a relief as soon as I can. Then you can take a year off for your honeymoon."

"Get along to Antofagasta yourself," Del advised him. "I've resigned."

"Don't talk to me like that, son! You know I've always depended on you. You wouldn't aim to bring my grey hairs down with sorrow to the grave. What would you like for a wedding present?"

The cheque-book came out.

Del laughed. "Put that away," he said. "There's nothing I want that I haven't got."

The wedding was on the day fixed for the opening of the Opera, and among the few guests was the former Inspector Chavez, now Assistant Commissioner of Police at Trajano, and the father of eight daughters. In the evening Don Sebastian sang Mario's final aria with so much heart-broken emotion that the audience brought him back from the grave to sing it again.

Next day Beckett Wayne returned to New York and the bridal couple flew south to Antofagasta. Lewis went back to the Casa Alta alone.

"I have finished my work," Señor Rivas told him. "There can be no definite proof that your brother was murdered, but I cannot see that it matters, since Izarbarra is dead and it is more than likely that Larreta was killed in the final bombing of the plateau."

Lewis made no reply.

"What is important is that all our other suspicions have been confirmed," Rivas went on. "Leite Mayorga was never your brother's wife, and it is clear that he did not know what he was doing when he signed the will."

Lewis nodded. Money had been made available and he had transferred funds to Talliver, but he was indifferent to what had happened or might happen in London. Nothing was important except the whereabouts of Leite.

"Why do you worry about the woman?" Rivas demanded. "She was the willing accomplice of Izarbarra. She is no good."

Perhaps he was right.

Pepe was back at the Casa Alta, still a little weak, but as cheerful as ever.

"I do not care what anyone says," he asserted. "She is good and brave. She is a fool, of course, but what woman isn't? I hope she is safe. I hope you will find her, Don Lewis. She will make you very happy."

All Don Lewis could find was the telephone number of the Casa Arenales.

"I wish to speak to Doña Maria Josefa," he said.

"Señora Mayorga is not available," a voice answered. "If you have any business with her, you must apply to Police Headquarters, Trajano."

House arrest! Still *incommunicado*.

The red cherries of the coffee trees were being picked day by day, and there were new problems of handling and marketing.

"Have no worry, Don Lewis," Pepe said. "I know what has to be done. I will attend to everything."

This was the opportunity to talk to Pepe. "I must go back to London very soon," Lewis told him. "Do you think you'll be able to look after the finca?"

"If you wish to trust me." Pepe was quite confident.

"There is no one I would rather trust. You will manage the house and the coffee. The lawyer will look after the rest. I shall come back to see you within a year, I hope."

It was the right thing; an appointment that Julian had once considered. "If I ever retire," he had said, "Pepe will carry on for me."

The material reward was discussed. There would be a commission on results as well as a substantial salary. Everything was settled, but Lewis stayed on.

Surely some word would come from Leite; at least a letter to tell him that she was alive, even if she had no wish to see him again.

A letter came from Anne. Del hoped to finish his work in Chile in another month. Then they would go to New York for a few weeks before crossing the Atlantic for a prolonged stay in Europe. "I can't tell you how we both look forward to seeing you in London, for surely you will be back home by then."

The letter was full of affection for him, but Del's name cropped up in every second line, and the more he read, the more Lewis was aware of his loneliness. Nothing was left of the daughter he had known. He was glad of her happiness, but it would be a long time before he was reconciled to the loss of her.

Great rain-heads were piling up over the mountains as he looked out from the glass wall of the solana. He heard a faint whisper of tyres on the gravel, but took no notice. Many cars came and went these days, for it seemed that everyone in the Government wanted to inspect the old Indian mine. But this time he was in request.

Pepe's voice, modulated to a quiet reverence, sounded in the corridor. The door of the sun-parlour was opened, and Lewis started as he saw the tall figure of a very old woman on the threshold.

"Señor Page, you will forgive this intrusion, I pray."

The thin voice crackled like static electricity, the small black eyes peered as the sharp, eagle-beak nose was thrust towards him. He wanted to cry out how welcome she was, but he could produce no more than an inaudible stammer.

Doña Maria Josefa came stiffly into the solana, her white-haired head nodding, the ferrule of her stick tapping on the tiled floor. Lewis moved a chair for her and held out an unsteady hand to assist her.

"Please give an order that we are not to be disturbed," she said. "I would have called on you sooner. This is the first day I have been permitted to leave my house."

She twisted in her chair and swivelled her head to make sure that the door was closed.

He asked urgently: "What has happened to Leite, madame? Do you know where she is?"

"I know that she is safe. I would ask you to be patient with an old woman, señor. I have come to you because of Leite. I wish to make an explanation."

He saw that she was in some distress; short of breath, as though the walk from the car to the solana had been a little too much for her.

"Please take your time, madame," he said. "I will order maté. Or perhaps you will take something else?"

"I will take nothing, señor. I thank you for your kindness. It is not my hour for maté. Will you not sit?"

He brought a chair close to her and waited.

"You have, no doubt, a poor opinion of the Mayorgas, señor, but I have not come to make excuses. In San Mateo political fanaticism has often led to excesses, and these excesses have bred more fanaticism. My niece has been a victim of this national malady."

"Madame, I ask you to believe –"

"Please don't interrupt me, señor. Night after night I have rehearsed what I must say to you, and I beg you to listen. The government of Enrique Bartol was not a good government. He was a weak man, easily led by evil counsel. When he was overthrown, we had for a while a reign of terror. I do not blame Recalde for this. Any man may be compelled by circumstance."

She looked towards the great window as the first drops of rain splashed on the glass.

"Any man may make mistakes," she went on. "Leite's father was arrested. He was accused of treason and shot without a trial. He had the misfortune to be the stepfather of Pascual Izarbarra and he paid for that with his life. He was a wealthy man, an owner of wide lands. His wealth and lands were confiscated. His daughter had to go into exile because, as a university student, she had identified herself with the Bartolistas. A schoolgirl, señor! A stupid, unfledged schoolgirl who did not know her own mind."

Maria Josefa closed her eyes and shook her head sadly. When she looked again at Lewis her face was hard.

"After that, she knew her mind. The instinct for vengeance is a primitive thing, señor. The civilised may reprehend it, but it is difficult to shake off. Leite had been devoted to her father."

"This is unnecessary, madame," Lewis protested. "I quite understand."

"But you must understand everything. She was ready, when the time came, to enter into any conspiracy for the overthrow of Recalde. And the time came. I was not aware of all that was going on here, any more than she was when she returned. She was asked to play wife to a dying man so that funds could be secured for the return of Bartol. She knew it was to be robbery, but she saw it as a necessary political expedient. Do you understand that?"

"I assure you that you have no need to pain yourself."

"The victim was a foreigner, an exploiter of San Mateo. And San Mateo owed her great estates and much wealth. She was only too ready to be the dupe of her half-brother, and it was not for some time after she arrived here that she became fully aware of the reality. You know that reality, señor. You helped her to see it. More than that, you helped her to see herself."

"All this is unimportant, madame." Lewis stood before her, pleading. "I wish only to find her."

"To find her?" The quick dark eyes blinked at him. "You would find her very changed, señor. She is cured, yes. She wishes never to see San Mateo again. She has gone back to her exile, a hard world for her. She is bitterly ashamed, and must do penance."

"Then you will tell me where she is?"

"I am sorry. That she forbids. I have come to you only because she does not want you to think too badly of her. Now, if you will permit me, I will go back to my house."

The world he saw was darker than the rain-clouds could make it.

Assisting her, he held her arm as the stick tapped on the tiles. He prayed and argued, but always she shook her head. When she was seated in her car, he stood in the rain, holding the door open, still pleading.

"I will write that I have seen you," Maria Josefa said. "But for your own sake, señor, you must forget that Leite Mayorga has any existence."

The rain pattered thinly in great stinging drops as the car moved off. He saw the grim face of the old woman as she stared forward at the back of the chauffeur's neck. He stood motionless, watching the receding car, and he was unaware of the rain. He turned and saw Pepe standing in the doorway.

"Look!" Pepe said. "The car is coming back. Doña Maria Josefa must have forgotten something."

Lewis looked in dejection. The rain was heavier, throwing a veil over the gods and warriors at the end of the forecourt. The big car wheeled round the drive, the tyres crunching the wet gravel.

"I have changed my mind," Maria Josefa said. "I have decided that Leite has another lesson to learn. She is a silly child, yet a man like you, Don Lewis, could make a woman of her. For a few more days she will be in Panama, at Colon. Here is the address. Perhaps you are a fool, but that is God's business."

He took the card, then leaned into the car and kissed her hand.

In another moment he was at the telephone, trying to reduce his voice to something less than a shout.

"Hello! Pan-American? I want a seat on the first available flight to Cristobal . . . To-morrow? Wonderful! That's wonderful!"

ERIC AMBLER

Doctor Frigo ISBN: 978-07551-2381-0

A coup d'etat in a Caribbean state causes a political storm in the region and even the seemingly impassive and impersonal Doctor Castillo, nicknamed Doctor Frigo, cannot escape the consequences. As things heat up, Frigo finds that both his profession and life are horribly at risk.

'As subtle, clever and complex as always' - Sunday Telegraph

'The book is a triumph' - Sunday Times

Judgment on Deltchev ISBN: 978-07551-1762-8

Foster is hired to cover the trial of Deltchev, who is accused of treason for allegedly being a member of the sinister and secretive Brotherhood and preparing a plot to assassinate the head of state whilst President of the Agrarian Socialist Party and member of the Provisional Government. It is assumed to be a show trial, but when Foster encounters Madame Deltchev the plot thickens, with his and other lives in danger ....

'The maestro is back again, with all his sinister magic intact' - The New York Times

The Maras Affair ISBN: 978-07551-1764-2

(Ambler originally writing as Eliot Reed with Charles Rodda)

Charles Burton, journalist, cannot get work past Iron Curtain censors and knows he should leave the country. However, he is in love with his secretary, Anna Maras, and she is in danger. Then the President is assassinated and one of Burton's office workers is found dead. He decides to smuggle Anna out of the country, but her reluctance impedes him, as does being sought by secret police and counter-revolutionaries alike.

Eric Ambler

The Schirmer Inheritance   ISBN: 978-07551-1765-9

Former bomber pilot George Carey becomes a lawyer and his first job with a Philadelphia firm looks tedious - he is asked to read through a large quantity of files to ensure nothing has been missed in an inheritance case where there is no traceable heir. His discoveries, however, lead to unforeseen adventures and real danger in post war Greece.

'Ambler towers over most of his newer imitators' - Los Angeles Times

'Ambler may well be the best writer of suspense stories .. He is the master craftsman' - Life

Topkapi (The Light of Day)   ISBN: 978-07551-1768-0

Arthur Simpson is a petty thief who is discovered stealing from a hotel room. His victim, however, turns out to be a criminal in a league well above his own and Simpson is blackmailed into smuggling arms into Turkey for use in a major jewel robbery. The Turkish police, however, discover the arms and he is further 'blackmailed' by them into spying on the 'gang' - or must rot in a Turkish jail. However, agreeing to help brings even greater danger ....

'Ambler is incapable of writing a dull paragraph' - The Sunday Times

ERIC AMBLER

Siege at the Villa Lipp (Send No More Roses)
ISBN: 978-07551-1766-6
Professor Krom believes Paul Firman, alias Oberholzer, is one of those criminals who keep a low profile and are just too clever to get caught. Firman, rich and somewhat shady, agrees to be interviewed in his villa on the French Riviera. But events take an unexpected turn and perhaps there is even someone else artfully hiding in the deep background?

'One of Ambler's most ambitious and best' - The Observer

'Ambler has done it again ... deliciously plausible' - The Guardian

The Levanter
ISBN: 978-07551-1941-7
Michael Howell lives the good life in Syria, just three years after the six day war. He has several highly profitable business interests and an Italian office manager who is also his mistress. However, the discovery that his factories are being used as a base by the Palestine Action Force changes everything - he is in extreme danger with nowhere to run ...

'The foremost thriller writer of our time' - Sunday Times

'Our greatest thriller writer' - Graham Greene

Made in the USA
Monee, IL
20 July 2020

05